'What changed your mind? Party for one not satisfying, huh?'

'The party hasn't started yet.'

His voice took on a persuasive tone that brushed over her skin like velvet. He seemed to draw something from her that she'd never known she had. Was she out of her depth with this one?

'Do you think I'm going to abandon my hostess responsibilities for a frolic across the sheets with you?'

He raised a dark brow. 'Are you?'

The scary thing was she had a feeling that was exactly what was going to happen.

He closed the door, muting the sound of the party below.

She clutched the edge of the dressing table on either side of her hips. If she touched him she might not be responsible for her actions, and with him she very much needed to be responsible.

His head dipped…his mouth hovered. 'I'll admit to a little curiosity of my own,' he murmured, and touched his lips to hers.

Dear Reader

Brie's story hadn't fully formed in my mind when I began writing my last book, MISTLETOE NOT REQUIRED, where Brie makes her first appearance. Brie supported her friend Olivia when she had to make some heart-wrenching decisions. Likewise, Olivia was there for Brie as Brie struggled to improve her relationship with her long-lost brother, Jett.

Because that's what friends are for.

From the start, Olivia's party-loving friend was demanding to be noticed—so much so that I had to promise her a book of her own, and here it is.

Digging into Brie's past to find out why she's such an attention-seeker was the fun part—giving her a worthy opponent even more so.

Leo Hamilton is a short-term, casual kind of guy when it comes to women and relationships. His brutal past and consequent responsibilities have made him a bit of a control freak, and this aspect of his personality immediately clashes with Brie's sassy independence.

He's also a man of integrity—as Brie is about to find out for herself...

Anne

THE PARTY DARE

BY
ANNE OLIVER

First published in Great Britain 2014
by Mills & Boon, an imprint of Harlequin (UK) Limited,
Eton House, 18-24 Paradise Road, Richmond, Surrey, TW9 1SR

© 2014 Anne Oliver

ISBN: 978-0-263-24294-2

Anne Oliver lives in Adelaide, South Australia, and with its perfect location and relaxed lifestyle why would she want to leave?

In another life Anne was an early childhood teacher, but not long after she began writing paranormal and time travel adventures as a weekend escape she knew it was more than a hobby. Eventually preferring the fun of writing contemporary romance, she dreamed of swapping yard duties for the life of a published author.

It happened in December 2005, when she was accepted by Mills & Boon® for their Modern Heat™ series. The dream continued when her first two published novels won the Romance Writers of Australia's Romantic Book of the Year in 2007 and 2008. She considers herself very lucky to have been a finalist for the same award in 2012 and 2013.

Other interests include animal welfare and conservation, quilting, astronomy, all things Scottish, and eating anything she doesn't have to cook.

Visit Anne at her website: www.anne-oliver.com

Other Modern Tempted™ titles by Anne Oliver:

MISTLETOE NOT REQUIRED

DEDICATION

To make a friend you first have to be one.

With thanks to my critique partners:
Kathy, Linda, Lynn and Suzie.

Thanks also to my editor, Meg Lewis,
who read the story and asked the right questions.

CHAPTER ONE

'I SHOULD FOREWARN you the purchaser intends to renovate. Big time.'

'Renovate? *Big* time?' Breanna Black blinked at her soon-to-be departing next-door neighbour, Carol. 'Do you know what that involves, exactly?'

'I overheard elevator and wall demolition to make way for indoor pool mentioned. Amongst other things.'

The words were still echoing in Brie's head at Carol and George's farewell dinner more than twenty-four hours later. She shook her head as she rinsed her hands in Carol's upstairs bathroom. The Reece-Bartons had sold their beautiful mansion, East Wind, to a moron. East Wind was a mirror image of Brie's West Wind next door, built by brothers in the late nineteenth century. Obviously Leo Hamilton—her new *clueless* neighbour—didn't appreciate historical structures or their significance. She swiped up the hand towel, rubbing away at the excess energy she didn't know what to do with. *An indoor pool?* For heaven's sake. If he wanted—

'Apologies for the interruption, George.' An unfamiliar voice drifted up the stairs. 'I didn't realise you had company.'

Deep and rich and silky, the timbre seemed to harmonise with the foyer's warm wood-panelled walls where she imagined the recent arrival standing. Pushing the bath-

room door wider, she cocked an ear in the direction of the
stairwell and listened.

The actual words were muffled by the flautist's rendi-
tion of "Greensleeves" and the disorder of mingled con-
versations from the twenty or so guests, but it was the tone
that hooked her attention. Would he look as scrumptious
as he sounded? she wondered. A shiver of lust shimmied
down her spine. Would he sound the same in bed?

Then George and his visitor moved from the foyer, their
voices merging with those at the dinner party.

Wow. Brie straightened away from the wall she'd been
leaning against and moved to the mirror. She hoped he'd
stay for a drink at least so she could get a gander at him
but she took her time repairing her make-up, determined
not to give in to temptation and rush downstairs merely
to satisfy her curiosity. Whoever he was.

Finally, she slid her lip-gloss into her purse and exited
the bathroom. He was probably married with six kids.
Except he didn't sound married. 'And what exactly does
married sound like?' she scoffed out loud. He had to be
short, then—being six foot tall herself had its disadvan-
tages. Except she couldn't imagine anyone with a voice
like that being anything but…

Perfect.

He appeared on the top stair as if she'd conjured him
up, and her normally forthright and confident 'Hi' turned
into a breathless schoolgirl sound of awe and appreciation.

He gave a brief half-nod. Said, 'Evening,' in that sexy
as sin voice. One hand on the newel post, he stepped onto
the upstairs landing. Thirtyish. Tall. Taller than her. Close-
cropped dark hair, steel-grey eyes. Whipcord lean and
tanned—her idea of a perfect man in one succinct pack-
age from his clean-shaven jaw to his crisp white business
shirt and twilight-blue tie to his perfectly pressed charcoal
trousers…with security pass clipped to his belt.

Leo Hamilton.

She almost groaned aloud. Perfect to look at but sadly that was where it ended.

Her smile remained frozen in half bloom on her lips. She refused to be seduced by his better than gorgeous looks. Beauty was only skin deep after all. Wasn't it great timing that she'd just fixed her lip-gloss? She frowned at the ridiculous thought that popped up from nowhere. *No.* It wasn't great at all.

What she really wanted to do was tell him exactly where to stick his renovation ideas. But she straightened slowly, drew in air tinged with the faint scent of skin-warmed cotton and reminded herself there was nothing to be gained by rudeness. *Pull yourself together, Brie. Smile. Forget those pesky little renovations he's planning and try the neighbourly, welcoming approach.*

To start with at least.

'Mr Hamilton. I couldn't help but notice your name.' *Oh...* Wrong place to look. She gave a little shrug—*wrong place to wear it*—and dragged her eyes from his crotch and up to meet his grey impenetrable ones. 'I'm Breanna Black.' She stepped forward, stuck out her hand. 'Your next-door neighbour.'

He nodded, all unsmiling and enigmatic. 'Breanna.' He took so long to extend his own, Brie wondered for a moment if he intended responding at all.

When he did, at last, take her hand in a decisive grip, she didn't reciprocate like some weak-willed female meeting her teenage idol but with the same strength and intensity as he. He looked startled. His eyes widened and his jaw tightened and she got an impression of hard, wide, slightly roughened palm before he released her. Or had she pulled free first?

Whatever, that first contact was as brief as it was disconcerting so she followed up quickly with, 'Call me Brie.

I've heard you're moving here from Melbourne?' *And a few other not so good things besides.*

'It's more of an investment, but yes. You heard correctly.' The way he said that last, almost accusatory, made it sound as if she were the town busybody when *he* was the ignoramus with no appreciation for history or architecture. And okay, she was interested only because he was going to be living next door—*and renovating*—which might affect the property value of her own home.

'Bad week at the office?' she murmured. 'Thank God it's Friday?' When he simply stared at her and made no attempt to reply, Brie continued, 'Carol told me. That you're from the mainland.' She defended what she considered her reasonable query, even if he did not. 'She and George are more friends than neighbours. So, you've big plans for this place?' The words shot out before she could stop them. 'An indoor pool, I hear?'

'Do you believe everything you hear?'

His cool stare matched his barely veiled criticism then he glanced down the stairwell, giving her time to check out his profile. The neat shape of his ear, the pinprick of evening stubble along the sharp jawline. Her trained therapist's eye couldn't help but notice his suntanned skin would benefit from one of her men's all-fruit facials, and her mouth tingled at the errant thought of licking it off— *Stop.*

She pressed her lips together. Unlike the Reece-Bartons, this man was *not* her friend. In any way. If she could just convince her woman's body of that fact. 'Not at all, but I believe Carol. Are you aware that this home is a signific—?'

'Chris, up here.' He raised a hand to some unseen body below, effectively cutting Brie off.

The lifelong sense of powerlessness she'd always felt at being repeatedly ignored bristled along her spine. *'Excuse me?'*

His focus turned sharply and wholly back to Brie. She wasn't being ignored now and the words she'd been about to say melted off her tongue. They stood almost eye to eye. Mouth to mouth. Breast to chest. Her nipples tightened. So did her belly. Somehow he made her feel dainty and petite, an achievement no man had ever accomplished. His gaze seemed to check her out from the roots of her hair to her low-heeled boots and every place between.

'My architect,' he said, finally.

Architect. Chris. Right. Now she had his attention back, she struggled to regather the thread of their conversation. 'What does he think of your plans?'

But she was suddenly speaking to empty space because, without a second glance, he was headed back the way he'd come, his masculine scent drifting on the air behind him.

Rude. Inexcusably, unjustifiably rude. Brie saw a blonde clutching a tablet device to her ample bosom, which was plumped over an inappropriately low neckline. She watched the woman move to meet him at the foot of the stairs. His architect. Female. Of course. He actually smiled at the woman and Brie fought a stab of pique. He wasn't ignoring *Chris.*

She watched them compare notes, converse a moment, then George appeared and both men walked towards the front door while Chris and her tablet headed towards the kitchen. The guys shook hands but just when Brie thought he'd forgotten she'd ever existed, Leo Hamilton turned his head and that enigmatic silver gaze found her, skimming her entire body again.

Her skin prickled, as if he'd given her an all-over body scrub with one of her salon's best exfoliating mitts. She shivered and resisted the urge to soothe her arms.

A corner of his mouth lifted. A smile? Or a smirk... As if he knew the effect he'd had on her. She narrowed her eyes. Damn. She was a confident woman when it came to any man, hunky or otherwise, so why this particular man wielded that power she had no idea—he was irritating and arrogant and dismissive. And a bunch of other things she refused to waste her time thinking about.

If he began to raise his hand in some sort of belated farewell, she didn't see it. Eyes averted and head high, she started downstairs. She heard the front door close and aimed a smile George's way. 'I hope I didn't scare him off.'

'I'd venture your new neighbour's not a man who scares easily,' he said, returning her smile. 'He had a plane to catch.' George fell into step beside her as they headed back to the dinner table. 'You'll have plenty of time to get acquainted,' he said with the devil in his voice.

A half-laugh caught in her overheated throat and she had to clear it. 'He's not my type.'

'No?'

'No.' Granted, conservative senior citizen George probably thought every man was her type since he'd probably never seen her turn into her driveway with the same guy twice.

But he'd be wrong. She enjoyed men but she was discerning in her choice of partners. The arrogant guy next door with the mellow bedroom voice? No way.

She shook off the double distraction of Leo Hamilton and her bedroom in the same image. Apart from finding out what his intentions were for East Wind—which she could do by talking with his architect if necessary—she couldn't wait to ignore him the next time she saw him.

Leo leaned back against the prestige cab's headrest as they headed for the airport. What the hell had happened back there? His whole body was still vibrating, as if he'd been blasted sideways by a sonic boom.

The after-effects of the shockwave that was Breanna Black.

His libido had jolted awake and demanded breakfast, an occurrence so unexpected and so irrational given his usual taste in women that he'd left Chris with the calculations he'd intended checking through alongside her.

He barely noticed Hobart's lights winking as he crossed the Tasman Bridge. A neighbour who could light his fire with just a look was a complication he didn't need. Perhaps he could oversee what needed to be done via email? He dismissed that idea with an impatient snap of fingers against his thigh—this project was as personal as it was important.

Whereas *she* wasn't important. In any way. He refused to alter his plans on a woman's account. Particularly one he'd just met.

And now he was going to be at the airport half an hour earlier than planned where he'd no doubt spend that time digging her out from beneath his skin.

He didn't have time for the attraction. The distraction. Or whatever the hell Breanna Black was.

Still, if he had to choose one word to describe her it would be stunning. Not in the usual way one called a woman stunning but in a stun-gun kind of way—and he was still feeling the burn.

She was all about impact rather than beauty. There was nothing subtle about her. Her cheekbones were too wide and too sharp for her face. Then there was the eye-popping lime tasselled top that stretched taut over firm, round and very generous breasts. Her mouth...ripe and red and damned if he hadn't wanted to move in and—

He closed his eyes but the woman's image blistered the back of his eyelids. Her hair a shiny river of blackberry silk flowing over her shoulders. Midnight eyes flashing with an inner fire, which made him wonder if that apparent passion for knowing other people's business extended to her bedroom.

Leo pinched the bridge of his nose to alleviate the tension building between his brows. He wasn't being entirely fair. Breanna had introduced herself at least, whereas he'd not exactly been Mr Congeniality.

Nice work, Hamilton. Way to antagonise the new neighbour. His sister needed an ally in this new community—another woman she could rely on when he wasn't around—not an adversary.

So he wouldn't be telling Sunny about bumping into Ms Black yet, he decided. If he happened to see Breanna next weekend—and he didn't intend going out of his way to do so, but if he did—he'd make more of an effort. For Sunny's sake.

Two hours later the Melbourne night wrapped its chill around his bones as he jogged up the shallow stone stairs of home. The evocative strains of violin drifted from within. Sunny was weaving her magic and he listened with brotherly pride. Little wonder she'd been accepted into Hope Strings, which performed as part of Tasmania's prestigious Philharmonic Orchestra, and at the ripe old age of twenty-four.

Rose and amber light spilled through the front door's stained glass, and as he pushed it open the delicious aroma of Mrs Jackson's slow-cooked bouillabaisse filled the air. His highly valued daytime housekeeper, and worth every cent he paid her.

He shrugged out of his coat and paused, a feeling of warmth seeping through him. Unlike his childhood, these days coming home gave him a comforting sense of peace and achievement.

But circumstances were about to change yet again. With Sunny's exciting new career taking off, despite her physical challenges, his little sister had demanded her independence. In no time at all, she'd be in her own home, in a new state. Alone. She'd point-blank refused his offer to employ a live-in housekeeper but had agreed to a cleaner on the condition she paid the woman's wages herself.

He zoned out and let the violin's sweet melancholy wash over him. *Enjoy the moment while you can.*

The house fire had robbed Sunny of the use of her now withered right leg and deformed foot, but had that slowed her down? Not on your life. If anything it had made her stronger, more determined.

She'd have that autonomy with his blessing—and some conditions. He'd arranged to install a personal emergency alarm system and insisted she wear a distress pendant at all times while in the house. And—*yes, Ms Black*—he had indeed checked out the feasibility of a pool.

Tasmania's climate didn't favour an outdoor construction, so he'd been considering alternatives. Sunny loved swimming; she found the weightlessness liberating. But not when she was alone. Which was why, in the end, he'd decided against the pool. It wasn't in keeping with the home and he didn't trust her to stay away from a pool when he wasn't there.

His freelance environmental management consultancy business took him to Tasmania on a regular basis and he anticipated dropping by her place at every opportunity. He also intended purchasing a suitable apartment nearby for himself. She could yell *control freak* and *uncompromising jerk* as often and loudly as she liked—he was immune as far as her insults were concerned, and was more than comfortable with any label she threw at him so long as she was safe.

'Why are you standing there all by yourself and looking like the world's about to end?'

'Hey, Suns.' He realised he'd been lost in thought awhile. 'I was listening to you play and thinking how quiet it's going to be here.'

'Doesn't say much for my skills then; I stopped five minutes ago.' She was leaning on her elbow crutch in a slant of light studying him with a half-smile on her lips, blonde hair curling in wisps around her face.

He nodded, coming out of what felt like a daze. 'I'll want a CD of your music.' He was going to miss her. Sunny by name, Sunny by nature.

'Already working on it.' She cocked her head. 'Problem with the new house?'

Why did her question immediately conjure a certain dark-haired dynamo rather than his latest property acquisition? 'A few surprises, that's all.'

That famous Sunny mood dimmed. 'So there *is* a problem.'

'Nothing I can't handle.' He walked to her, clasped her shoulders with both hands and smiled his reassurance. 'I'm ravenous. Did you wait for me?'

'Of course I did.'

He squeezed her shoulders and released her, and she accompanied him down the passage, her crutch tapping lightly on the tiles. They both preferred the cosiness of the little kitchen alcove over the formal dining room. Because he knew she wanted him to, Leo sat down and let her ladle the fish stew into two bowls without assistance.

She'd raided his wine stash. He poured two glasses of pinot noir from the bottle she'd set on the lace-cloth-covered table. 'Celebrating again?'

'Can't seem to stop,' she said with a laugh. The table was arranged flush against the bench to accommodate Sunny's disability and she carried the bowls to the table one at a time. When she was seated, she raised her glass. 'To the next adventure.'

Crystal chimed against crystal. 'Wherever it is you'll find it, Suns.'

'I was thinking more along the lines of *your* next adventure.' Her blue-eyed matchmaking gaze winked back at him.

He leaned back and studied his glass. 'We seem to be talking at cross purposes again.'

'What happened with that pretty little brunette you sent fifty red roses to then escorted to the theatre last month? Aisha, wasn't it?'

Ah, Aisha. Perfectly lovely, perfectly amenable. Or so he'd thought until she'd expected him to pay the cancellation fees for the overseas honeymoon she'd booked in anticipation of his marriage proposal.

Sunny and his love interests were very separate aspects of his life, except that she'd caught him ordering the roses. 'You know me.' He broke open his bread roll. 'Short-term casual all the way.'

'You're right, I *do* know you. And it's just sad.' She pointed an accusatory finger at him then shrugged and sighed rather dramatically. 'Okay, so you're looking for ways to make your next million.'

'Accumulating wealth.' He drank deeply then tilted his glass towards her. 'I thrive on the challenge.'

She grinned, picked up her spoon. 'I love a challenge too. Swimming in the Australia Day Big Swim on Sydney Harbour, for instance.'

Leo set his glass down and blinked at her while she tucked into her meal. 'Are you serious?'

'I've put my name on the list for swimmers with disabilities,' she said around a mouthful of fish. 'January's nine months away. Plenty of time for you to agree to be my swim buddy.'

'We'll need to have that conversation at some point,' he growled and got stuck into his own meal. But of course he'd agree—what was more, she knew it.

She tolerated her scars and deformity without a whisper of complaint or self-pity. Her wish to live independently was her choice, not his.

'I'll be fine,' she said, reading his mind.

'Mum would've been proud of you.'

'She'd have been proud of *us*.' Spoon halfway to her mouth, Sunny eyeballed him. 'I know what you're thinking. Don't.'

Sunny's pain was physical and would last a lifetime. Leo's anguish was deep and every bit as enduring. Guilt. Regret. His memories of the night twelve years ago when their lives had changed forever was as stark and real and terrifying as if it had happened yesterday.

He'd saved his sister but had been too late to pull their bruised and battered mother from their burning home. If his father hadn't goaded him into swinging that punch earlier in the evening, maybe the monster wouldn't have come back later and torched the place. The only justice was that he'd also died in the blaze.

'I wish she could have been here to see me perform in Sydney,' Sunny was saying. 'She'd always wanted to attend a concert at the Opera House.'

'*I'll* be there,' he said, pushing the past away and raising his glass to her.

'I'm counting on it. It's my last gig with the gang before I join Hope Strings. Three weeks, don't forget.'

'I won't,' he promised.

How could he forget? He only had to oversee the renovations, secure his own rental accommodation in Hobart and check out the environmental practices of a new client on the east coast of Tasmania in addition to his existing workload.

And to top it off there was the nosy neighbour with the attitude.

He tossed back the last drop of wine and set his glass

on the table with a decisive *plunk*. He absolutely, positively, without a doubt, didn't have time for a distraction like Breanna Black.

CHAPTER TWO

ONE WEEK LATER on Saturday afternoon, with Eve's Naturally closed for the rest of weekend, Brie made her way to East Wind's back door trailing her small plant trolley. She and Carol had exchanged keys years ago for those times when either of them were away. Before she handed her key to the agent Monday morning, she'd made arrangements to reclaim several dozen potted herbs and flowers she'd given Carol over the years. She'd intended collecting them during the week but had been working insane hours and they'd slipped her mind.

Taking a last look down the driveway to make sure Mr Hamilton of the husky voice hadn't decided to turn up in the last two minutes, she deactivated the alarm and let herself in. Not that she expected him—apparently he wasn't able to collect the keys until Tuesday. Carol hadn't elaborated and Brie was thrilled with herself for not asking for more details.

The glass-walled atrium formed a semicircular structure at the back of the home; soothing and familiar scents greeted her as she crossed its old brick floor. The sun's warmth on nutrient-rich, damp soil. Basil. Oregano, mint and lemongrass. 'Hello, my little treasures.' She trailed her fingers over a variegated thyme. 'I've come to take you home.'

Positioning the trolley near the workbench, she collected

the smaller pots, and to keep the more delicate plants going until she had time to deal with them tomorrow, she filled a spray bottle and began misting them.

She caressed the thick leaves of a large aloe vera in an elegant waist-high blue pot. 'You're going to be a challenge to lift, aren't you, my pretty? Maybe I should ask our friendly as a frozen fish neighbour for help.'

Huffing out a breath, she plugged her ear buds into the smartphone in the hip pocket of her jeans, switched on her favourite playlist. 'He'd have to acknowledge I'm alive first.' In time with her music, she shot off three hard squirts at a struggling coriander. 'And I sure as heck am not going to be first to acknowledge *him*.'

He'd barely given her the time of day. As if she'd been invisible.

Story of her life.

Well, not quite. She knew she stood out in a crowd *now*, thanks to her late growth spurt at the age of fifteen. She'd had years to practise how to garner attention—and she'd learned well. Even if it hadn't always been attention garnered for the right reasons and had landed her in trouble more often than she cared to remember. Her rebellious years.

These days she didn't have to work hard for that attention. Except from people like Leo Hamilton. And why did that irk her?

'I'm very much alive, Mr Big, Bad and Built,' she told an overgrown cactus with delusions of its own importance. 'And I'm going to make it my business to show you I *do* exist.'

Aiming her bottle at it, she squeezed the trigger. Hard. Seemed she wasn't done with rebellion yet.

Arms crossed beside a potted kumquat tree, Leo leaned a shoulder against the door jamb and watched with some amusement while his new neighbour drowned the arid-loving cactus and his reputation as a usually well-mannered guy. With those bits of plastic in her ears, he wondered if she even knew she was voicing her opinions aloud. Yeah—she existed all too clearly and, despite his best efforts to the contrary, his body responded, the tension tightening with every squeeze of her slender fingers on that trigger bottle.

He wasn't hiding but he was counting on her not seeing him just yet—he hadn't witnessed anything as fascinating as Breanna Black making herself at home in *his* atrium since his pubescent self had ogled the naked female form for the first time.

He'd wandered around the back of the house with some landscaping ideas on paper to find the door open. He was ticked off that she still had the key George had mentioned and, worse, she was still using it. Obviously she had the security code as well. He intended familiarising her with the concept of privacy...soon. Right now he couldn't take his eyes off her. She had the sexiest backside, especially when she wiggled it as she was doing now in time to music only she could hear.

Her top was a yellow-raincoat yellow, and, from what he could see in profile as she moved, cling wrapped to those abundant breasts. The short hem flared over black leggings that clung to long, long legs. She looked like the sunflower she was standing next to.

She continued squirting, flicked her long black plait back over her shoulder. His fingers itched to free it from the confines of its elastic band, to watch it shimmer the way it had that moment at the top of the stairs last week, to feel its silky texture against his palms. To bring it to his nose and inhale. Slowly. Deeply.

Pull yourself together.

She was a neighbour, and, right now, a damn nuisance. He'd worked past midnight every evening this week so he could be in Hobart over the weekend to check out some nearby short-term accommodation for himself while the electrician ripped out the guts of this place and installed new wiring throughout. The plumbers were going to be here, and the kitchen renovation crew.

He did not want this woman in his space. Nor did he need her sensual perfume wafting his way and clogging up his sinuses with scents better appreciated in the bedroom.

She plunked the sunflower on the trolley, gave it a drenching. 'He'd better not be planning any external changes that will affect the value of *my* home. An elevator, for crying out loud? And if he even thinks about getting rid of that foyer chandelier...' Her rant trailed off—presumably she was contemplating what she'd do to him in the event.

Wearing skin-tight leather and brandishing a whip.

The image of the two of them engaged in bodily combat flashed before him. The slippery slide of that black leather against his flesh. His teeth finding the vulnerable place under her chin while she screamed in pleasure. He clenched his jaw—he could literally feel his blood pressure spike.

He'd heard enough. He wanted her out of here, now. Before he said, or did, something detrimental to his state of solitary well-being.

Uncrossing his arms, he pushed off the door frame.

'Now why would I want to do that?'

The low murmur near her ear at the same instant someone removed her ear buds had Brie practically leaping out of her skin. 'What the...?' Fists raised, she spun around. *'You.'* Her fists uncurled and she lowered her arms to the workbench. 'You startled me.'

She was still startled, but in an electrifying, breath-stealing way, and her strength seemed to drain out of her under the force of his steely eyed gaze.

He wore casual today—faded denim and a matching soft-looking jumper, and he smelled of warm wool and that indefinable masculine scent she recognised from the last time she'd seen him.

'Then again, if I did want to do that…' He didn't appear concerned that he'd scared ten years off her life and looked her up and down in a manner that wiped whatever she had been talking about from her mind.

'Do…*what*? And…and what are you *doing* here?'

'Shouldn't I be asking you that question?' His voice was all reason and calm. Not to mention husky and low and seductive.

'I thought George told you about the key,' she went on, since she did owe him an explanation. 'And the plants.' She began picking up pots at random, setting them on the trolley. 'I apologise, I meant to get around to it during the week but I was busy.'

One dark brow rose, his expression clear. *Doing what?*

'You're not the only one who works, Mr Hamilton.'

He slouched casually against the workbench. 'You can rest easy—I have no intention of removing the chandelier. The elevator's not happening and there'll be no exterior changes—I love the house's old-world charm and I appreciate that the two buildings share a history, which I believe should be retained. Apart from some electrical and plumbing work, I'm doing some kitchen renovations, which involve shifting a wall about fifty centimetres, but they won't compromise the integrity of the place. You okay with that?'

She breathed a sigh of relief and slapped a hand to her chest. 'Thank goodness. I've been thinking about you— about *it*—about your *renovations* all week.' *Busted.* 'And I've been thinking other stuff out loud too, haven't I?'

No reply as his gaze stroked over her again.

Her blood rushed through her body and heat bloomed beneath her skin. 'I'll, um, get out of your way.' She tossed the rest of the pots onto the trolley willy-nilly. When had she ever been so scatter-brained talking to a man?

'You wanted me to give you a hand with this one, right?' He indicated the aloe vera.

He gave no outward hint that he'd heard her 'friendly as a frozen fish neighbour' comment, but she knew he had, and cringed inwardly. 'That'd be great,' she muttered. 'Thanks.'

'Reckon you'll need to keep it steady,' he said, lifting it on board the trolley as if it weighed no more than an empty bucket. Which drew her attention to the movement of the muscles beneath his jumper. The way they stretched the wool tight across his chest and bunched beneath the sleeves.

He glanced her way. 'Your back yard, I presume?'

She shifted her focus to his eyes. *Only* his eyes. 'No need for you to bother. I can manage, thank you.'

'Wouldn't want that pot to shatter.'

Wouldn't want her self-control to shatter either. She wanted to be away from him asap. Away from his warm man smell that made her want to burrow against his chest and breathe deep. She didn't *want* to like her new neighbour but her body had a mind of its own.

Best to let him play Mr Macho then and get it over with. Get *him* over with and she could go back to whatever she'd been doing before. If she could just remember. 'Okay. Thanks.'

They proceeded outside with rattling pots and trailing greenery as he manoeuvred the trolley towards the driveway.

Probably not wise to tell him she'd entered his property this way but, 'There's a gap between our fences.' Brie lifted a chin in the general direction, holding the pot steady with both hands. 'Carol and I used it to save time. I was going to close it after I got the plants,' she told him.

When he said nothing, she continued, 'We looked out for each other. As neighbours should. Don't you agree?'

'I'd say it depends on the neighbour.' They reached the gap and he stopped to inspect it. 'I'll organise a tradesman.'

'Fine. Thanks.' He seemed so keen to take charge, she'd let him. *This* time.

'Which reminds me.' He held out his hand, palm up. 'You have my key.'

Brie glimpsed scarring on the inside of his forearm as she retrieved the key from inside an empty ceramic pot and dropped it in his palm. 'Thanks, it'll save me a trip to the agent.' Flipping her hand, she grinned at him. 'And while you're at it, you might want to change the security code.'

'Yes. I will.'

Then he smiled back. Kind of. As if he hadn't meant to and it was a surprise to him too, generous lips quirking at the corners. She glimpsed a twinkle of humour in his eyes.

Her stomach fizzed, her limbs went soft and her fingers tightened on the rim of the pot as her inner flirt demanded she come out and play. *No*, Brie told her.

He looked away, resumed pushing the trolley again. 'So, Ms Black. Breanna—'

'Brie.'

'Brie. How do you earn a living?'

'I'm a beauty therapist. You?'

'Environmental management consulting.'

Her brows lifted. 'And what does an environmental management consultant do, exactly?'

'I freelance to businesses who want advice on their environmental practices.'

'You must charge a fortune for your services.' She gestured towards her garden shed as they crossed the square of lawn bordered by recycled pink bricks. 'You might as well know I'm a tell-it-as-it-is kind of girl—I know how much you paid for the place.'

He cleared his throat. 'My clients seek me out, not the other way around.'

'Really? With those interpersonal skills I witnessed last week?'

'I was in a hurry.'

'Because of me?'

He made a strangled sound, cleared his throat again. 'No excuses. I apologise.'

Hmm, uncomfortable. How charmingly appealing. She loved having that effect on a man. Her resolve to keep her distance was weakening by the second. 'Accepted. You had a plane to catch, right?'

'Correct.'

'And a date waiting?'

'Not precisely. Are you always this…?' He seemed to struggle for the word.

'Straightforward?' Not the word he'd have used, she'd wager, and his 'not precisely' answer clarified nothing. 'Pretty much. You mentioned this was an investment, so will you be here often?'

They stopped at the shed and unloaded the pots.

'I'll be stopping by to check on the progress. And I've just taken on some new clients in Tasmania so I'll be on the island most of the time. Where do you want the aloe vera?'

'Inside the conservatory. Thanks.'

She watched him push the trolley to the rear of the house, then, once inside, she helped him unload the pot where she wanted it. 'Would you like something to drink? I have a chilled fruit tisane in the fridge.'

He regarded her blankly. 'Thanks, but no thanks.'

'Sure? It's a very refreshing beverage.'

'I'm a coffee man, myself. And I'm due to check out

some rental accommodation in the Arcade Apartments.'
He checked his watch, displaying a thick wrist dusted with
dark hair. 'Twenty minutes ago.' Grimacing, he yanked out
his phone, sent a voice message apologising and advising
he'd make a time later this afternoon.

Millionaire's accommodation, the Arcade. 'Where are
you staying at the moment?'

'A bed and breakfast two minutes away.'

She nodded. 'That'll be Hannah's Hideaway. How much
are you paying for an apartment at the Arcade?'

'More than it's worth.' He spoke briskly, pocketed his
phone with a similar movement. 'Proximity's important.'

Brie, always on the lookout for extra funds for Pink
Snowflake, came up with an instant light-bulb idea. 'How
long are you looking at?'

'Few weeks.' A tiny frown dug between his brows.
'Why?'

'What would you say to living right next door?'

'I'm not interested in a room.' Penetrating eyes considered hers and he took his time answering. 'If that's what
you're offering.'

'I'm not offering you a room.' She matched his gaze.
'My brother, Jett, and my best friend, Olivia, are on their
honeymoon and I'm house-sitting their new health retreat
from next week for a couple of months or thereabouts. It's
totally flexible. So, you could stay here, have the entire
place to yourself and the rent money could go to the Pink
Snowflake Foundation instead of the Arcade owner's over-
inflated bank account.' She grinned at her own ingenuity.
'It's win-win.'

'Hmm.' He squatted in front of the blue pot, tested its
stability on the uneven green tiles recycled from the sixties and laid with her own fair hands. 'What's the Pink
Snowflake Foundation?'

'Jett and Olivia are opening a luxury holistic retreat

for cancer patients to recuperate after their treatment and Pink Snowflake is Olivia's project of love that made the whole thing possible. It's ahead of schedule but the happy couple are overseas. They asked me if I'd like to spend a few nights a week there. Soak in the spa, enjoy the pool and solarium. Use the gym. Explore their private cellar. Naturally I couldn't refuse.'

'Naturally.' The tone was dry. Rising, he hooked his thumbs in his jeans pockets and looked about. 'You own this place? You live here alone?'

She nodded. 'I inherited it when my parents died and, yes, I live alone.'

'So I'd have the entire place to myself? No unexpected interruptions. Until the job's done?'

'All yours. Although I may need to come by and collect the odd outfit or whatever. But you'd have all the keys and I'd ring first. I wouldn't just drop in.' *Unless you invited me.*

As if he'd heard her private thought, his eyes dropped to her mouth. He looked away fast, checked his watch again and she pounced before he could refuse. 'When would you want it by?'

His eyes flicked back to hers. This time they held. 'Next weekend.'

Was it her imagination or was there something in the way he said that? A glint rapidly masked behind that quicksilver gaze?

'Sold,' she told him before she could think of all the reasons why inviting a man she knew nothing about—except that he turned her on—into her private sanctuary might be a bad idea. 'The Pink Snowflake Foundation thanks you.'

'Okay, we'll give it a try,' he said finally. 'I'm all for a good cause.' He pulled out his mobile, cancelled his appointment with the Arcade rep.

'"We" as in you and a partner?' Brie spoke more sharply than she meant to.

'"We" as in you and me.' The way he linked them together in that low, husky voice while he held her gaze prisoner made her pulse race with excitement. 'I want to see it,' he said, sliding his mobile back into his pocket. 'If it's not an inconvenience.'

'Not at all.' She gestured him towards the far side of the conservatory while she got herself under control. 'Family area's through here. Layout's the same as yours,' she said, whisking a basket of washing off the sofa as she passed. 'Have a seat and I'll get you a drink. I have fourteen kinds of tea, hot or cold— Oops, you're a coffee m—'

'Thanks, but there's no need,' she heard him say. 'I'm meeting my architect in ten.'

The busy blonde with the over-exposed boobs. 'Chris.' She raised a brow. 'Thought you weren't planning any major changes?'

'Just that kitchen wall I told you a...bout...' Leo's voice trailed off as he took in the visuals. He'd walked into chaos.

What appeared to be an entire wardrobe of party dresses was strewn across an armchair. As he entered the kitchen, a variety of foodstuffs covered every available surface but he had no idea what she intended cooking. He gave a mental shudder, comparing it with his own ordered world, from his computer files to his DVD collection to the way he arranged his ties.

Had she thought this idea through? He doubted it. By all appearances, it seemed she was one of those impulsive people who never stood still, gravitating from one interest to the next as the whim took her.

'Excuse the mess. I've been experimenting with some nature-based facial masks and steams.'

Which explained the bowl of pink mash that smelled like strawberries and peppermint. But not the fifty or so plastic beer and wine glasses stacked alongside a large box of Moroccan lanterns. 'I'll come back later,' he told her. When he'd reconsidered.

'Hey, if you're in a hurry now, why don't you come by this evening? I'm having a party—ten o'clock on—you could check out the place then.'

Fine for some. He had a Saturday night date with his laptop. To ease the pain, he was planning to help the evening along with a nice Tasmanian Cabernet Shiraz. He intended stopping at the trendy upmarket bottle shop he'd seen nearby. But that wasn't the only reason. An evening with Breanna Black in party mode was a bad idea. 'No can do. I've got work to finish.'

'Don't we all? But on a Saturday night?' She clucked her tongue. 'That's just sad.'

'Some might say so.' But he was proud of his consultancy business. His alone. He'd built it from the ground up, with nothing but determination and hard work and it was the first and only part of his life he'd ever had absolute control over. It was worth a few sacrifices.

'I'll leave you my contact number.' He placed his business card next to a row of a dozen or so unusual teapots on a distressed wood sideboard then turned to her. 'If you'll tell me your details, I'll come by tomorrow. I'm presuming afternoon'll be best?'

She smiled. A naughty smile that seemed to make him an accomplice in whatever racy plans she had for the evening, and almost had him wishing he'd accepted her invitation, bad idea or not.

Temptation beckoned with the luscious curve of those full lips. 'Give me your phone.'

Holding out her hand, she stepped close. Too close, and into his personal space. Feminine scent enveloped him; the tips of her extended fingers brushed his jumper.

He stepped back. She wasn't getting her hands near

his contacts list—or anywhere else for that matter. His groin tightened at the erotic thought. 'Just tell me, I'll remember.' He had an exceptional memory for numbers and facts—except right now he was having trouble remembering his own name.

She rattled off a series of numbers as he walked to the door.

'We'll work out the details tomorrow,' he muttered.

He didn't stop till he reached the new SUV he'd picked up only hours ago. Sliding onto the caramel-soft seat, he tipped his head back and closed his eyes, lust and frustration building a fire below his belt.

Hadn't he stayed away from her? Minded his own business?

Had it made a scrap of difference?

The woman wasn't merely a nuisance, she should come with a warning label. *Approach at your own peril.*

So much for working without being disturbed. Brie didn't have to be physically present to mess with his head.

Tonight was going to be a long, uncomfortable night.

CHAPTER THREE

BRIE, AN EXPERIENCED hostess, was running late for her own party. Her plant rescue expedition had taken longer than she'd anticipated. The reason for that was an enormously sexy man and he was still centre stage in her thoughts. And didn't she love the fact that here was a man who more than matched her height? She set out nibbles, arranged tea-lights and lanterns for lighting later while she thought about her impulsive offer to rent her home to him.

She doubted he'd expect the use of the entire house but it was going to be a race against time to have the place tidy and the stuff she wanted to take to the retreat packed by next weekend. On top of that, the thought of Leo Hamilton sleeping in her bed, on her sheets, sent a shiver through her, along with the question: did he sleep naked? There was no alternative. It was the only room with a bed long enough and wide enough to accommodate a man his size.

Two hours before her guests were due to arrive, she drove to the liquor shop. She'd paid for her order, the cartons already stacked in her car with a friendly staff member's assistance, when she remembered she'd intended to buy a bottle of sparkly to enjoy after work in the retreat's spa later in the week.

And there he was, the most recent object of her private fantasies perusing the classiest labels in the red wine section. Labels so out of her price range, she could only imagine the smooth, rich flavour. No doubt the two of them had vastly different tastes. And not only in wine.

Come on, Brie, when has that stopped you?

It might be fun at that.

She picked up the nearest bottle of sparkling white while she watched him from the corner of her eye. She'd glimpsed a sense of humour this afternoon. Even traded flirty looks with him. Whether he acknowledged it or not, Brie knew when a guy was interested.

She also knew that the moment the renovations were done, he'd leave the property in his agent's hands and move on to his next million-dollar investment. He was that kind of guy. She smiled to herself. And *that* made him the perfect kind of guy—perfectly constructed, perfectly casual, perfectly short-term.

When Brie set her sights on a man, he didn't stand a chance. But their fun times never lasted long—these days she made sure of it. Since Elliot, her motto was *no heart, no hurt.* Worked for her every time.

Heat stroked Leo's left cheek like a glove and the hairs on the back of his neck seemed to move antenna-like in the same direction.

He knew why before he looked up.

He'd seen Breanna and her puppy-dog assistant stacking up her car with booze and thought she'd left. But no, she was walking towards him, holding a bottle of bubbly and wielding her flirtatious smile like a challenge. His fingers tightened on his two-hundred-dollar bottle of Barossa shiraz cabernet and, with a vague nod towards her, he moved to the refrigerator section.

Like an inevitability, she kept coming. He selected a black olive pâté and his favourite cheese—a Tasmanian Brie—before he realised the irony of his choice.

Too late to swap for a Camembert. Was this some kind of cosmic conspiracy?

She'd loosened her hair and it slid over her shoulders, straight and thick and glorious. She stopped in front of him, noted his product choices and wielded that smile some more. 'Party for one?'

'Might as well get some enjoyment out of the evening while I work.'

She flicked her hair back in an artful, well-practised feminine move. 'Why do tonight what you can put off till tomorrow? I have some crackers at home that would go nicely with that Brie.' Her eyes seemed to say *the type of cracker that goes off with a bang.*

'I'm sure you do. *Brie.*' He refused to be seduced by her smoky-voiced invitation with its barely subtle innuendo. To prove it, he maintained his nonchalant gaze towards her as he drew out his wallet. He was all in favour of seduction, but he wanted to be the one doing the seducing. Wherever and whenever *he* was good and ready. He ignored the fire in his chinos insisting that time was fast approaching. 'I'll see you tomorrow afternoon. As arranged.'

'Fine,' she said, not looking away. 'However you want to play.'

Hard and fast. The unspoken words singed the air between them.

He waited for Breanna to break the searing eye contact first. The tension stretched out for several long seconds. Only when she finally glanced at her watch then delved into her bag for her purse did he turn towards the cash register at the end of the aisle.

'Afraid you might enjoy yourself, Mr Hamilton?' she teased behind him. 'Or is it me you're afraid of.' It wasn't a question.

He turned, caught her teasing, tossed it back. 'Not at all. Parties aren't my scene. Too many people.' He intentionally lowered his tone. 'But a party for two...' He watched the teasing light in her eyes flare to frank awareness and a distinct attraction before she looked away. Score two to him.

I'm as eager to find out as you are, baby doll. But he had no intention of acting on it. Yet. *He'd* decide the if and when and it wouldn't be tonight. Still, he couldn't help grinning as he walked to the counter and set his platinum card down.

She followed, stood a good arm's distance along the counter from him, considering the bottle in her hands. 'I think I'm going to need two or more of these,' she murmured to herself.

'Best to be prepared, I say.'

That startled a laugh out of her. 'You're not what I expected, Mr Hamilton.'

'Should I interpret that as a good thing?'

'I'll let you know. Later.' She dared him with a hot glint in her midnight eyes, a quick curve of those glossy lips.

Which had him wondering how those eyes would look dazed with passion, how her lips would feel pressed against his own. How they'd feel against other body parts...

He gritted his teeth as his body responded to that tempting glimpse of paradise. He refused to be dictated to by his hormones. Or Ms Black. Swinging away, he raised his bottle in farewell as he moved to the door. 'Enjoy your party.'

Yanking open his car door, he shook his head. Unbelievable. He was walking away from an opportunity to share the evening with a hot woman who obviously wanted the same thing he did.

He slid inside, sat a moment, staring through the windscreen. His next-door neighbour. Correction: *Sunny's* neighbour. She and his sister looked about the same age, had the same feisty personalities—they'd probably get on well, even long-term.

Whereas he and Breanna? It would be hot and temporary, like that firecracker she'd made him think of. A whizz-bang, short-term fling.

But unlike the easy-going, casual women he hooked up with, this one would clash plenty with him. Give him a whole lot of drama he didn't need.

He'd endured more than his share of emotional trauma. As a kid hearing his mother's broken pleas when her violent husband exercised his conjugal rights and slapped her around while doing it, her sobs in the dark after he'd gone.

For more than half his lifetime he'd been powerless to change the situation. And every time his young self had tried, his mother had copped the beatings and the bruises.

Then there was the fire. Sunny's arduous recovery and rehab. The relentless questions that nagged at him: what could he have done differently? What *should* he have done to change the outcome?

His breath fogged up the windscreen and he swiped a hand over the glass, switched on the ignition. High drama? Not him. No way. He'd planned his evening—a meal in one of the city's upmarket restaurants overlooking Sullivans Cove, a few hours of work in the cosy sitting room accompanied by his favourite shiraz. Nothing and, more specifically, *no one* was going to interfere with those plans.

At ten-thirty, Leo powered off his laptop and stretched cramped muscles. The decision to postpone opening his wine had given him a clear head to work. His latest client was a new six-star eco lodge on Tasmania's east coast with the beguiling name of Heaven. He'd finished reading their initial commentary and had noted his suggested changes and added his in-depth report an hour earlier than he'd anticipated.

It left him at a loose end for the rest of the evening.

Was that why he'd subconsciously postponed opening the bottle in the first place? Frowning, he dismissed it.

He never felt the need to self-analyse. Until tonight. Until Breanna had burst into his life.

Her name alone brought her to sparkling life behind his eyes in a thousand different images, like seeing her through a kaleidoscope. Each one bright and sassy and unique.

Unsettling.

He paced to the window, stared past the rain pattering lightly on the night-darkened glass, in the direction of their homes, a two-minute drive away. He'd seen a substantial amount of liquor ferried to her car this afternoon. Was that a regular thing? He drummed his fingers on the pane. She was obviously a girl who enjoyed fun times. Were her parties noisy and boozy and out of control?

Tonight was an ideal opportunity to check things out and ensure his latest and most important acquisition was in Sunny's best interests. It wasn't as if he hadn't been invited, he reminded himself, and, picking up his bottle, he grabbed his car's remote.

The unmistakable sounds of revelry greeted his ears when Leo strode up Breanna's rain-slicked path with his bottle of wine a short time later. Bass thumped. Loud, but not loud enough to intrude on her neighbours' peace. It scored Breanna a conditional nod of approval, even if her taste in music did nothing for him.

It appeared to be an open-door policy so he let himself in, crossed the foyer lit by a chandelier that matched his own. As he stepped into the formal lounge room, the atmosphere, overly warm with too many bodies packed into one place, enveloped him. Glow from the Moroccan lanterns splashed the shadowy room with splotches of orange and watermelon pink.

He waited for his eyes to adjust, expecting to see Breanna standing tall amongst the crowd wearing some eye-popping creation. Guests were gyrating in time to the pounding beat, others were loading plates at the spicy-smelling buffet in the corner.

But he didn't see Breanna. He exhaled on an impatient breath. Where was she?

An attractive redhead in a slinky purple number found her way through the dancers and bobbed up in front of him. 'Hi.'

Her smile was friendly interest. He was surprised to find it did nothing for him. 'Hi there,' he said, only half listening while he continued to search out the only reason he was here.

'I'm Samantha. We haven't met, have we?'

'No, we haven't. I'm Leo.' He nodded towards the empty wine glass she was caressing. 'Where can I get a couple of those?'

'Drinks? I'd love—'

'Glasses.' He held up his bottle. 'You don't know where Breanna is, do you?'

'She's not far—I saw her a few moments ago talking with Bronwyn.' Her smile evaporated and she waved towards the kitchen. 'Glasses are that way.'

'Thanks.'

On the lookout for the hostess, he made his way through the crowd, grabbing two clean long-stemmed wine glasses from the kitchen. The room looked marginally tidier than it had this afternoon. He spied a gaggle of girls in the family area where clothes had been scattered earlier, but saw neither Breanna nor her clothes. He checked the atrium where guests talked over booze and chips. The downstairs loo.

With the rest of the rooms in darkness, their doors shut, he presumed they were off-limits. Which left the next floor.

Familiar with the layout of his own place, he walked straight towards the master bedroom. He knew Breanna must be there since it was the only room with a light on.

The sensual fragrance he'd come to associate with her—
the one he'd taken to calling midnight temptation—drifted
in the air. Anticipation swarmed through him and his pulse
quickened.

He could hear movement and tapped on the semi-open
door. 'Breanna.' When there was no reply, only a fast rus-
tling sound, he tapped again. He was impatient to see her
now he was here. 'Breanna. Are you decent in there?' In
that instant it occurred to him that she might not be alone.
Something hooked in his gut. Was that what he'd heard—
two desperate would-be lovers trying to cover up fast? The
thought of some other man touching her the way he'd been
thinking of touching her shocked him into movement and
he walked in without further preamble.

Leo was here? Brie scrambled up, tugged the hem of her
new vermilion dress down, her heart jack-hammering. She
swiped at a lock of hair that had fallen over her brow. He
was the *last* person she wanted to catch her on her hands
and knees searching under the bed for a DVD she'd bor-
rowed from Bron and forgotten about.

She'd almost composed herself in front of the mirror
when he entered *without* waiting for her invitation. Still,
she could hardly hurl accusations—the door was open and
he *had* asked permission. She'd just chosen not to answer
until she was ready.

She still wasn't ready and her heart was still thump-
ing but she dragged her eyes to his reflection and locked
gazes with him in the mirror while her fingers fumbled
with the dress's neckline. She could almost see the heat
haze shimmering on the glass. Still watching his reflection, she saw him set his mega-expensive bottle of wine
and two glasses on her bedside table.

He wore black casual and oh…my. She didn't know
what possessed her but to demonstrate just how cool and

unruffled she was, not, she whirled around, sashayed over to him and planted a firm kiss on his mouth. Then she whirled back to the mirror.

Her lips were on fire. Her whole body was burning. She felt like a teenage rookie and glanced at him from beneath her lashes. *Think cool, think cool.*

He hadn't moved. He shook his head. 'What was that?'

She shrugged, the laugh catching in her throat. 'A whim. I was curious.'

Now she was even more curious. What would a full-on sensual assault be like? Trying for casual, she picked up her brush, ran it through her hair. Her arm felt strangely weak, as if she were coming down with a fever. 'What changed your mind?'

'I finished sooner than I expected.'

'Ah.' She nodded wisely. 'Party for one not satisfying, huh?'

'The party hasn't started yet.' His voice took on a persuasive tone that brushed over her skin like velvet. 'Nice.'

He meant her slinky dress—at least she thought he did—except his gaze seemed to skim only the bare thighs its short hem didn't cover, sending goosebumps over her flesh.

'Nice of you to notice.'

Setting her brush down, she turned from his reflection to look at the real man. And reminded herself to breathe. He seemed to draw something from her that she'd never known she had. Was she out of her depth with this one? 'Do you think I'm going to abandon my hostess responsibilities for a frolic across the sheets with you?'

He raised a dark brow. 'Are you?'

The scary thing was she had a feeling that was exactly what was going to happen. She loved playing the catch-me-if-you-can game almost as much as reaching the winning post but this time she seemed to be tied to the starting gate. 'You've got a high opinion of yourself, haven't you?' She wasn't going to make it easy for him.

He nodded. 'I'm comfortable with who I am. How about you?'

'At the moment I'm feeling pretty relaxed.' Not exactly answering his question. She smiled to hide the fact she was strung out like wet washing in the wind.

He closed the door, muting the sound of the party below. Taking his time, he peeled the foil off the top of the bottle, unscrewed the cap and splashed some wine into the bottom of the glasses. 'Do you like a good shiraz?'

'I do. I should—'

'This one's my favourite. I didn't expect to find it here.'

'Me either,' she murmured. She could delay her hostess duties a moment. Or possibly the rest of her life.

She leaned her backside against her dressing table for support as he stopped in front of her, both glasses in one large hand. The other he wrapped around the back of her neck, holding her skull in such a way so she was looking right at him. Up close his eyes were pewter flecked with cobalt. He smelled of fresh rain on cotton, shampoo and soap. She clutched the edge of the dressing table on either side of her hips. If she touched him, she might not be responsible for her actions, and, with him, she very much needed to be responsible.

His head dipped, his mouth hovered. 'I'll admit to a little curiosity of my own,' he murmured and touched his lips to hers.

Firm and warm. They moved gently; testing, teasing, tasting. Taking his time, showing her how devastating one long, drawn-out kiss could be. How a woman could be seduced into forgetting her own identity. Her fingers tightened on the wood behind her. She could feel his body heat radiating between them and her fingers itched to explore but still she didn't touch him.

She'd never been one for slow. This leisurely pace was new. Mesmerising. As her body melted against his her blood grew sluggish and flowed like clotted cream through her veins.

Even the sound of the rain on her window faded and all she was aware of were his fingers massaging the back of her scalp, his lips on hers, and the rich, dark promise of more. She yearned. When he raised his head, she bit back a sigh.

He lifted his hand from the back of her skull to trace a path just once down the side of her face, fingertips leaving a trail of tingling nerve endings. 'Breanna.' He slid his thumb over her bottom lip then took a step back.

He looked bemused, she thought. The way she felt right now. 'That was…that's a lot of curiosity.'

He reached out, flicked a strand of hair behind her ear. 'Unlike your "whim", I enjoy taking my time.'

'I noticed,' she said, feeling as if she were floating a few centimetres off the floor. She struggled to rein in her far-flung thoughts and ground herself. 'There are at least fifty people downstairs who'll be wondering where I am.'

'They seem a pretty self-sufficient lot. Try this.' He handed her a glass.

She took it with nerveless fingers and sipped, letting the rich mellowness caress the inside of her mouth. 'Mmm.'

He drank too. 'I doubt they'll notice you're missing for a little while.'

She sipped again. 'Someone could turn up here at any moment.' Bron, for instance.

'Does that bother you?'

'No.' It should, it really should but right now she couldn't bring herself to care. 'You're bad.'

He grinned, as if seducing women at their own parties was a regular pastime, and raised his glass. 'Your opinion?'

'Of the wine? Or the kiss?'

He watched her over the rim. 'We both know we enjoyed the kiss.'

He had that right and the knowledge shimmered through her. 'The wine's beautiful—smooth and rich.' *Like you.* Worth every cent he'd paid? Probably not. Still, she wasn't complaining and sipped some more.

But she'd not eaten since lunch and the wine's potency on an empty stomach spread through her limbs like an approaching anaesthetic. Her senses were filled with him, her mind reeling and already cloudy. Intoxication was a definite possibility and one she couldn't afford.

She set her glass on the dressing table. 'I'll just slip downstairs to check everything's okay and get us a dip and some of those crackers I promised you.'

Leo watched her slick a new layer of gloss over those luscious-tasting lips. He couldn't wait to muss her up some more. He wanted to see the real Brie first thing in the morning with no make-up and satisfied with a long, slow night of sex.

As if reading his thoughts, she grinned at him in the mirror. 'I'll be right back.'

As she crossed the plush sage carpet his eyes followed the sway of orange silk-clad hips and he imagined how those barely covered, shapely long legs would feel entwined with his.

Man, oh, man, he needed to sit down. He sank into a cream wicker rocking chair in the corner to wait for his body's response to partially subside—as if that were remotely possible. Not with Brie's midnight temptation fragrance permeating every corner of the room. The tantalising taste of her lips on his own. The girl knew how to kiss and no doubt a good deal more.

Taking a long, slow swallow of his drink, he focused on

the way it slid warm and satisfying down his throat rather than the *un*satisfying ache in his groin.

For his next distraction, he turned his attention to her bedroom. He'd expected something bold and out there like the woman herself but her room was feminine and whimsically romantic—if you ignored the shamble of clothes, paperbacks and boxes scattered every which way. Deep green walls showcased John Waterhouse prints—The Lady of Shalott, Narcissus and The Awakening of Adonis.

On the queen-size bed lay a heap of flamboyant outfits that looked as if they'd been tried on then hastily discarded. Beneath, he glimpsed a rose-coloured floral quilt. He stared in growing consternation. Was this the room she expected him to sleep in while he stayed here? This bed? Surely she had other rooms and other beds?

He ran a perplexed hand over his hair. He hadn't come here tonight with the intention of starting something with Breanna—his temporary landlady and Sunny's future friend.

His observations so far confirmed she was nothing like the type of women he enjoyed—soft, cuddly, *organised* women willing and happy to let him take control. Women who were aroused by dominant men.

So why the blazes would he want to start *anything* with Breanna Black?

He already had.

And why not? With a body like hers? Pushing up, he paced to the door, craned his neck to see if she was on her way. He couldn't wait to get her naked and beneath him and find out what really turned her on. Then set about driving her slowly mad with wanting it. Taking her to the brink of ecstasy with his hands and mouth, watching her eyes plead and burn with passion as he dragged her over the edge at last screaming his name—

Clenching his jaw, he checked the time. Where the hell

was she? She'd all but dared him to come to this bash
and he'd played right into her hands. With Breanna he
couldn't seem to think rationally. He was *still* playing into
her hands, waiting in her room like an obsessed fool until
she condescended to return. He shook his head to clear it.

She might have others fooled into playing her games,
but not Leo Hamilton.

It took a tall tumbler of iced water under bright kitchen
lights to clear Brie's cotton-wool head and remember that
she had a duty to all her guests, not just the man waiting
for her in her bedroom who did crazy things to her internal organs and just wanted sex.

'Hey, party babe.' Samantha popped her head around
the door. 'A guy was looking for you.' She gave the thumbs
up as she crossed the room. 'Did I forget to mention he
was pretty damn cute?'

Cute? 'He found me. Thanks. Would you take this to
the table, please?' Brie slid a plate of crackers with smoked
salmon pâté and dill out of the fridge. 'I'll be right back.'

'Take your time,' Sam told her, reaching for the platter
with a conspiratorial twinkle.

'I'll be right back,' Brie repeated firmly. There was
a party happening. *Her* party. *Her* friends. Her priority.

'Brie?'

She was halfway down the hall to invite the *cute* Mr
Hamilton downstairs to join the fun when the distressed
voice had her turning back. Megan swayed in front of her,
brow creased, lips white.

Brie gripped her friend's arms. 'What's wrong, honey?'

'I'm fighting a vicious migraine and the migraine's winning. I've been looking for you.'

'Oh, Megs, I'm so sorry.' Guilt crawled through her as
she propelled Megan to an unoccupied room off the hall,
pushed her gently onto the nearest armchair. Leaving the

light off, she squatted down in front of her. 'I'd invite you to sleep it off here, except the noise…'

Megan closed her eyes. 'Thanks but I need to go home before I throw up. Can you find Denis?'

'Sure.'

It took a few minutes to locate Megan's boyfriend having a smoke on the front veranda and a few more to help Megan to the car and see them off safely.

She was at the bottom of the stairs when Leo appeared at the top with that stern and uncompromising expression she'd seen him wearing last week. 'Hey, there. I—'

'We can make arrangements tomorrow,' he said as he descended. 'To work out the rental agreement.'

Had he added that last bit in case she thought he was referring to something more explicitly sexual when it clearly wasn't? Prepared to cut him some slack because she'd left him alone for longer than she'd meant to, she smiled, tried again. 'I'm sor—'

'Not too early, right?' he added, his eyes cool, shuttered. 'So you can party into the wee hours. Enjoy yourself.'

He hadn't given her a chance to explain. Hadn't bothered to hear her reasons, and he was leaving. Just like that. She clenched her fists against her sides. Let him think what he would—after a childhood of being a social outcast, she was done letting other people's assumptions and prejudices hurt her. 'Is this a bad habit of yours?'

'Is what?'

'Forget it, it's a waste of time.' She was doubly angry he could affect her to such an extent. *Why him?* she wanted to scream. When he reached the bottom of the stairs, she stepped in front of him and poked his chest with a finger. 'You know something? I *will* enjoy myself. They don't call me Party Babe Brie for nothing.'

Twisting away, she marched across the foyer, glared at him as she slipped off her shoes beneath the graceful

arch leading to the entertainment area. She ran her hands
down the sides of her dress in a deliberately provocative
manner that had the cool in his eyes turning molten, the
cobalt flecks darkening. So satisfying to watch that hand-
some jaw clench, as if he hated himself for responding.

She grinned. His fingers flexed at his sides. *Ooh,
yeah, baby. Gotcha.* Still watching him, she picked up
her strappy stilettos, spun them above her head. 'Hey, everyone, time to get this party swinging.'

CHAPTER FOUR

AT FIVE A.M. Sunday, with the last guest gone, Brie dragged her dance-weary feet upstairs to bed. A couple of hours' sleep... She blinked at Bron's DVD forgotten on the dressing table next to the half-empty bottle of shiraz. Leo Hamilton's fault.

She crossed to her en-suite bathroom and grimaced at what she saw in the mirror. Her make-up had worn off, leaving her skin pale and revealing darker than usual smudges beneath her eyes. 'One too many drinks, Party Babe Brie,' she told her reflection.

Her nightly cleansing ritual completed, she applied her own pre-mixed moisturiser then climbed into bed. She stared at the ceiling, wide awake, body still buzzing despite the fatigue. Her mind refused to shut down. Leo was no different from any other male in that he liked to look at the female form. Boys had started looking at her when she'd rivalled them in height during her fifteenth year and grown a pretty decent pair of boobs.

Which had hurt at the time because, in their twisted little adolescent minds, boys automatically thought she slept around. An easy lay, she'd heard Billy Swanson snigger before she'd decked him with her backpack. She still hated that men could enjoy a fling and were considered playboys or studs whereas women who enjoyed the same were gos-

siped about in less than flattering terms, but nowadays she
didn't let it get to her.

And nowadays mature men saw her as more than boobs
and legs—mostly. And if they didn't…did it matter? It
wasn't as if it was long term. And she enjoyed being in the
company of a nice-looking man. She enjoyed being swept
off her feet and wined and dined and danced. Most of all
she enjoyed how they made her feel at the end of the night.

She knew without any doubt at all that Leo could make
her feel *really, really* good. But unlike other men she'd
enjoyed spending time with, even hours after he'd gone,
Leo's potent energy lingered in her room and she dragged
the covers up over her face as if to shield herself against
its force and gritted her teeth.

Men. They filled a basic human need but, like parties
and new experiences, they were to be enjoyed and appreciated before moving on to the next. She was careful
to choose a partner on the same wavelength and with the
same expectations and moral code as herself. Cheating
was out. She never lied because she knew bitterly how it
felt to be lied to. She expected—no, she *demanded*—honesty in return.

Unstructured, temporary relationships were her thing.
Since Elliot. Eight years ago she'd been so dazzled by the
rich young executive she'd seen nothing but the stars he
hung in the sky exclusively for her pleasure. When he'd
started sending floral apologies for missed dates, she'd
made exceptions for him, and excuses. Until the stars had
faded and she'd seen him clearly for the lying, cheating
rat he was.

Leo's sudden arrival in her room had both surprised
and excited her, transporting her to another place with his
unexpected but fun spontaneity and slow-burning kiss.

Until it had ended in disaster less than fifteen minutes
later. How did he get away with his appalling lack of so-

cial skills? Yeah, looks and sex appeal—they worked every time. No, not every time and not with her. He had some major grovelling to do before she'd let him anywhere near her person again.

But she smiled into the darkness remembering his re-action on the stairs. Pure molten lust and powerless to act on it. Because, in that situation, *Brie* had held the power. For her, that power had been the only thing that had saved the moment. She fell asleep at last with the smile still on her lips.

While her raspberry mint tea steeped, Brie plodded outside with a carton of cans and bottles destined for recycling. She winced at the glare—nine a.m. on a Sunday morning was unspeakably early to be up after an all-nighter. But preferable to being assaulted with dreams of a man she didn't want to think about and whether he tasted as good in the morning as he had last night.

She emptied her recycling into the bin with a loud clanking of glass and metal.

'Good morning.'

The familiar voice resonated crisply in the chilly air. She swivelled to see the man himself watching her from the gap in the fence a few metres away. How dared he look so refreshed? So together? So attractive? Unlike the way she knew she looked without a scrap of make-up and less than three hours' sleep. 'We aren't meeting until this af-ternoon,' she said, turning her back to him. She gathered bottles from a patio table, tossed them in the bin.

'I was outside and heard you busy there. We could meet this morning if you prefer to get it out of the way.'

To avoid looking at him she wiped the table top with a rag and wished he'd go away so he wouldn't see her. 'This morning doesn't suit.'

He paused, obviously unused to people not falling in

with his plans. 'Okay. I've drawn up a schedule. Shouldn't take long. We can grab a coffee in town somewhere and work it out. Say one o'clock? I'm on the three-fifteen flight out.'

She rose, not avoiding his gaze now but looking him straight in those silvery eyes. 'I don't drink coffee. Work it out?' She said each word as if she were talking to a dim-witted child—which wasn't much of a stretch, considering last night's behaviour. 'Work what out, exactly?'

Genuine surprise crossed his expression. 'The details of the agreement you persuaded me was a win-win for both of us. Or have you forgotten already?'

'Ah. *That* agreement.' Temper seethed hot through her veins but she kept her cool. 'I thought you might be going to work on your apology for walking out last night without waiting for me to tell you that I was detained by a guest who'd been taken ill.' Brie waited a beat for that piece of information to sink in. 'This might be hard for a guy like you to comprehend but she took priority over anything you and I might have had going.'

At least he had enough smarts to look uncomfortable. 'Why didn't you say so last night?'

Incredible. 'You're making it *my* fault?'

He frowned. 'It's not about who's right or—'

She slammed the lid of the bin shut. 'Of course it's not.' A man like Leo was never wrong. 'Did you give me a chance to speak last night?'

A muscle popped in his jaw. 'Is she all right?'

'A migraine—she gets them sometimes. She'll be okay.'

'When you didn't come back I assumed—'

'Never assume, Leo.'

'Th— What's burning?' His voice sharpened, nostrils flaring, his head whipped towards her house. He didn't wait for a reply, pushing through the gap in the fence and hurtling towards the atrium.

In that instant Brie smelled it too and remembered. *'Omigod.'* She heard Leo's footsteps pounding behind her as she sprinted up the path and into the kitchen.

They arrived in the doorway together. On the stovetop flames licked the inside of her frying pan and acrid smoke billowed towards the ceiling. She froze for an instant, the terrifying crackling sound filling her ears as she tried to remember how to put out a grease fire.

In that same instant Leo's heart stopped and his mind spun back twelve years. Only for an instant but he saw it all, every last detail while he switched off the gas, grabbed Breanna's tea towels and shoved them under the tap. *Dragging Sunny from their burning home, the fallen beam trapping her leg as his mother screamed for help from inside the inferno. Impossibly far away.*

He relived it in horrifying and vivid Technicolor as he wrung the cloths out then laid them carefully over the pan. *Hands restraining him as he tried to go back inside for Mum, her screams lost in the commotion of falling debris and the wail of sirens.*

More smoke issued forth as the damp cloths snuffed the flames. The instinctive scream rising up his throat almost overwhelmed him, then he looked at Breanna, staring wide-eyed with shock at the blackened stove top. His first reaction—was this his fault for distracting her away from the kitchen? No. She'd broken a cardinal rule by turning on a frying pan and walking away. 'Are you okay?' he asked her.

'I will be. In a moment. Thank you.'

His nerves shattered, Leo scanned the ceiling, fear of what might have happened masked by anger. 'Where the *hell* is your smoke detector and why the *hell* wasn't it working?'

'There isn't one.'

'No smoke alarm.' He pressed his stinging eyes with the heels of his hands and ordered himself to simmer down. The muscles in his legs vibrated; his anger teetered on a dangerous edge. 'You're telling me there are no smoke alarms in this house?'

'Afraid not. I've been meaning to get around to it but—'

'You've been meaning to get around to it.' He lifted his gaze to hers, unable to believe what he was hearing. 'I don't suppose there's a fire extinguisher either?' When she shook her head he threw up his hands in frustration and shouted, 'So, what, you don't value your own life? Can't be bothered to keep yourself safe?'

'It's okay, the fire's out,' she said, waving an almost casual hand. 'You're overreacting to this whole thing. Of course I—'

'You have no *freaking* idea, do you? Not a bloody clue. Have you *seen* what burns can do to the human body?'

'N—'

'Obviously not.' Two strides, he gripped her upper arms. 'Woman, I could shake the living daylights out of you.'

She nodded like a puppet on a string. 'Okay, point taken. Can you let me go?'

What in hell was he doing? He released her so fast she almost stumbled back.

Blinking rapidly, she nodded again, glanced towards his scarred arm. 'I'm sorry. I've…you've…'

'No.' He stepped back. He loathed the fact that Breanna had witnessed his runaway outburst, and worse, that she'd been physically subjected to it. Emotional displays indicated a lack of control and, to his mind, constituted a weakness.

Leo Hamilton did *not* do emotion. He did *not* lose control. Forcing his gaze back to hers, he blew out a slow breath to steady himself. 'You sure you're okay?'

'I'm okay.'

Did he detect a bit of a wobble in her voice? For her own safety, he hoped so. 'Look, if I—'

'I got the message—smoke alarms are on top of my list.'

He wondered just how sincere that intention was. Easy to forget now that the emergency was over. Easy to forget if you'd never had a personal tragedy with fire. 'A change of plans.' He pulled out his phone, scrolled to her name. 'Tell me your email address and I'll send you the schedule I've drawn up. Let me know if there are any points you want to clarify. If not I'll see you next Saturday.'

She recited her address then added, 'No going out for coffee, then?'

Biting back a four-letter word, he shook his head. 'You don't drink coffee. Remember?' He slid his phone back into his pocket.

'You know what I mean. And I'm flexible—I can make an exception. For you.'

'Some other time.' He was still dealing with the stresses of the past few moments and the haunting memories they conjured up—he didn't want to deal with their attraction and Breanna's disturbing lack of concern at the same time.

A few seconds longer and it could have gone the other way. Chills chased down his spine and he knew he couldn't simply let it go. He strode to the door, let himself out, relieved she didn't try to follow.

Brie's legs shook so badly she slumped onto the nearest stool and closed her eyes. Her thoughts were on spin cycle and a swarm of bees buzzed in her ears. Now that Leo had gone she gave in to the shock of nearly setting her house on fire. Even worse; he'd seen it all—and saved the day.

Reaching for her teapot, she poured a mug with trembling fingers, barely managing to bring it to her mouth without sloshing it over the rim.

She'd like to think she'd have reacted with Leo's speed

and clarity. His scarred forearm—he'd had personal experience. Which was none of her business unless he chose to share it. Which he hadn't.

Forty-five minutes later she was scrubbing her grungy stove, still counting herself lucky, when she heard footsteps on the path. She heard a knock as Leo called her name and the sound of the screen door opening and closing.

He appeared in the doorway as she wiped her hands on a clean tea towel. She noticed how his frame seemed to block out most of the light and her heart pitter-pattered faster for the second time in an hour and for an entirely different reason. 'Did you forget something?'

'No. You did.'

Then she saw he carried a fire blanket still in its pack and an extinguisher under one arm.

'Is that to put out the sparks?' She knew it was a delayed shock reaction but she had the crazily inappropriate desire to laugh. 'You're hot, but not that h…' She trailed off beneath his steel gaze.

'Don't push me, Breanna. I'm not in the mood.'

She nodded, pressed her lips together briefly then said, 'Sorry. And thanks. Thanks heaps. I was trying to lighten the moment. Guess not, hey.'

Ignoring her response, he set his purchases on the table, scanned the kitchen walls. 'You got a couple of hooks? I can hang the blanket for you.'

'I can manage a couple of hooks. Really,' she said when he looked sceptical. 'I'll do it today, I promise. And thanks again, I mean it. How much do I owe you?'

'Don't worry about it.'

'But—'

'Buy me a drink some time.'

She might have taken him up on it, but he was already walking to the door.

In ten seconds flat he was gone. Back to Melbourne.

She wasn't disappointed, she told herself, unpacking the blanket. All work and no play wasn't her type. Busy business-focused men weren't her type. They'd drive each other mad; she had no doubts about that at all.

Still… She hugged the blanket to her chest, remembering that kiss last night. Wouldn't it be fun discovering if she was right?

She should have found him those damn hooks.

On Wednesday evening Brie noticed a light on next door as she pulled up in her driveway around six-thirty. Apprehensive, she squinted through the night-darkened foliage for a better view. It was way past business hours and Leo was still in Melbourne. At least, she presumed he was, and she felt a surprised little flutter at the possibility that he'd come back earlier than expected.

She was about to check whether his car was under the car port when a guy in overalls ambled up her drive. He raised a hand. 'Ms Black? Mr Hamilton told me to come.' He dug in his overall pocket, pulled out a piece of paper. 'Name's Trent Middleton and I'm installing a smoke alarm for you this evening.'

Brie frowned at the work order. 'I didn't order a smoke alarm.'

'It's all paid for, just needs installation. Mr Hamilton told me to wait till you came home.'

Had she missed a text or something? 'My goodness, how long have you been waiting?' She could have been gone for hours. What if she'd gone out for drinks or a movie? Had Leo even considered that?

Trent shrugged. 'Since four. He paid me to wait.' He grinned. Obviously being paid to do nothing suited him well.

Brie could hardly send him away now. 'You'd better come in, then.'

She didn't like that Leo had taken it on himself to install an alarm. Nor did she want to be beholden to him for the cost. Breanna Black paid her own way, thanks very much.

Leo was one of those men who needed to have a handle on every situation and took it as a personal failure if he didn't.

She didn't want him having a say in her personal circumstances, or her life if it came to that. But she couldn't pretend she didn't feel a warm fuzzy that he was concerned enough to do this for her.

So later that night when she climbed into bed, she called his mobile.

'Good evening, Breanna,' he answered over the distant sound of a television. There was an unexpected hint of relaxed in his usually laconic tone. 'I was expecting your call.'

Hearing his dark velvet voice close to her ear sent a rush of heat through her body. She tried not to imagine him lying next to her and saying much more interesting things into her ear and said, 'So you know I'm a well-mannered person who always says thank you.'

'You're welcome.'

'You should also know I don't accept charity.'

'Wasn't charity, Breanna. A fire alarm's mandatory for residential rentals. As a property owner, you—'

'Enough said.' She waved a hand in empty space. 'I'll be reimbursing you for the cost if you'll send me the invoice. I'm making it clear right now, I pay my own way.'

There was a pause. 'So you'd be the type of woman who likes to lead on the dance floor.'

'For your info, when I'm on it, I *own* the dance floor,' she informed him. 'And you'd be the type of man who likes a woman to lie back in bed and let you do all the work.' She switched off her night light, stretched out on her crisp cotton sheets and indulged in the tempting image.

'We seem to have shifted from dance floor to bedroom in rapid succession,' he said, sounding amused. 'You want to test that theory of yours, Breanna?'

'I'm a direct kind of woman, so I might. But we were talking about fire alarms and the paying of them. Business is business and, as your landlady, I get to reimburse you.'

'We'll toss for it, then. Winner pays for the alarm. You call, I toss.'

'No deal.' She laughed. 'You think I'm that gullible?'

'I'll text you a photo of the result.'

'R-i-i-ght.'

'Okay. Something else.' The sound of the TV faded as if he was moving to another location. 'I'm home, are you?'

'Yes. What something else?'

For some reason she imagined him settled in a large wingback chair in front of a roaring fire with a brandy. Her pulse stepping up, her mind already a million miles ahead. She could do a lot with that big chair and brandy scenario...

'Three statements about yourself. One's a lie. I guess which one, then it's your turn.'

Could be interesting. 'Okay.'

'First to get three wrong...'

But Brie didn't hear the rest because her focus had shifted to the female voice that suddenly piped up in the background. She couldn't make out the words but it hardly mattered: He was chatting up one woman on the phone while entertaining another in his home. No wonder he'd moved to another room to talk. *Sucked in, Brie.*

She sat bolt upright. 'One, I'm twenty-six. Two, I've circumnavigated the earth in my bi-plane. Three, I'm not interested—and I'll give you a hint: *that's* not the lie.' She stabbed a finger in the air. 'I don't play those kinds of games.' Pressing the disconnect button, she glared at the dim light coming from the window, furious with him, furious with herself for being so easily manipulated. Again. Hadn't Elliot taught her anything?

She absolutely refused to admit to being disappointed. This thing with Leo was only a flirtation. And now it was over.

When the phone buzzed a moment later, with his name on the screen, she ignored it. The next time his name popped up she muted all calls, tossed the phone onto her bedside table with a clatter and rolled over. The way she always handled unwanted calls.

Nobody lied to Brie and got away with it. Not any more. She wished Leo Hamilton to the bottom of the Pacific Ocean.

CHAPTER FIVE

BRIE STILL WISHED Leo Hamilton to the bottom of the ocean the following morning. He wouldn't have still been on her contacts list but for the fact that he owned the house next door and she was darn well going to pay him for his darn fire alarm.

So she was beyond angry with herself when she answered her phone the following day during her lunch break without checking the screen and heard his voice in her ear.

'*Don't* cut me off.'

Her finger hovered over End Call. How creative a liar was he? 'You've got ten seconds.'

'I've figured out why you—'

'Five.'

'Sunny's my sister.'

'Your sister was with you last night?' Brie laughed. 'You think I'm that naïve?'

'No, but it's the truth—we share a house.'

'You share a house with your *sister*?' He'd mentioned a sister. She really wanted to believe that he was telling the truth. But… 'Why?' What was wrong with him that he'd share a house with his sister?

She thought she heard him hesitate, then he said, 'It's a big house. Our separate living areas are off-limits to the other unless invited and we meet on neutral grounds in the kitchen for meals.'

'You'd better not be lying.'

'Why would I lie to you?'

'Oh, I don't know, why would you?' *How about because you only have to smile or say one word and I want to believe everything you say*? Just as she had with Elliot. Maybe she had to start giving guys a chance. It was too depressing to believe they were all Elliots.

His rich low chuckle flowed around her like melted chocolate. 'I'm curious, Brie. Were you jealous?'

She rubbed a hand over the place where her heart had skipped a huge beat and coughed out a laugh. 'You called me Brie.'

'I guess I did.' He sounded surprised. 'So, were you?'

'Jealous? I wouldn't go that far.' *Moving right along.* 'I've read your email.' She picked up a sandwich triangle but didn't eat it. 'I looked over your schedule and everything seems to be in order.'

'Yes. You indicated as much in your emailed reply twenty-four hours ago. You don't remember?'

Oh. 'I only wondered if a busy man such as yourself would find time to check all his emails.'

'If I didn't, I wouldn't have a business, would I?'

'Right. Well.' She checked the time and composed herself. 'I run a business too. My next appointment's a chest and back wax then I have an aromatherapy treatment and two Brazilians and I haven't finished my lunch—'

'Chest and back wax,' he repeated, seemingly stuck on that next appointment.

'Yep.' She bit into her sandwich, spoke around it. 'Huge, hairy, masculine—you get the picture.'

There was a choking sound followed by, 'I'll let you get on with it, then.'

He disconnected and Brie grinned, popped the rest of her sandwich in her mouth and went to check the temperature of her wax.

* * *

On Saturday afternoon Leo strolled around the corner and into West Wind's back yard and did a double take. Breanna's face was caked with a layer of dark mud, her hair swathed in a magenta terry-towel turban while she massaged some product into her toes, the nails of which were an electric blue. She wore maroon leggings under a loose green shirt.

He'd known it was a useless exercise over the rock beat hammering away inside her house, but he'd rung the front door bell anyway then sent her a text. She'd answered neither, so he'd made his way around the back to the atrium.

Leo preferred to think she'd simply lost track of the hour but it seemed more probable she'd forgotten he was coming today. The more he looked, the more likely it seemed she'd forgotten he was coming at all. She was wearing those ear buds again—in addition to her sound system— and there was no sign of any packing or urgency to do so. As he drew closer he saw that the wrought-iron table was covered in little make-up pots and bowls along with a tall jug full of cubes of watermelon and lemon slices and a bowl of chocolate mousse.

Just another casual Saturday afternoon prepping for the next social event on her calendar? *Party babe Brie,* she'd informed him last weekend, sassy-mouthed as Scarlett O'Hara on steroids. And tonight was Saturday night, after all.

Leo didn't know what irritated him more: the fact that he'd been looking forward to this afternoon more than she obviously had or that she'd not even bothered to organise this arrangement that she'd suggested in the first place.

When he stopped in front of her, she glanced up, screamed and yanked out her ear buds at the same time. Her horror-stricken expression made him grin. 'If it isn't the party princess.'

'Party princess?' Covering her lower face with her hands, she glared up at him with those gorgeous black-as-midnight eyes and spoke through her fingers. 'Why do you have a problem with that? I have a social life even if you don't and you weren't due till *tomorrow*. Why do you have to keep sneaking around and startling me?'

'I tried the doorbell, and sent you a text. Our agreement was Saturday; you *did* read the schedule—didn't you? And I distinctly recall mentioning Saturday the last time I saw you. In your kitchen. Remember? Pan on fire, no smoke alarm? That day.'

Oh peachy. Just peachy. Brie wanted to go some place dark and hide for the next twenty years. 'You said a lot that morning but I don't remember you saying Saturday,' she said from behind her hands while she rose, stepped into her shoes.

'It's on the schedule,' he informed her, obviously enjoying her discomfort. He had a twinkle in his eye as he spoke. At least she *thought* he did—she wasn't looking too closely.

He waved an all-encompassing hand. 'And I seriously doubt you'd have been ready by tomorrow in any case, judging by this confusion.'

She'd been testing her products before using them on her clients, and of all the days to get carried away, when a silver-eyed hunk in tight black jeans, snowy open-necked shirt and tan jacket came to tell her she'd misread his precious schedule.

'Probably not,' she admitted, struggling to keep it together. 'I've been busy and a bit distracted this week.'

He gave an almost imperceptible nod, which had her wondering if he'd been distracted too, and for the same reason, then he grinned again and said, 'By the way, mud's a good look for you.'

'Is that supposed to be a compliment?' she snapped. Embarrassment prickled and she was sure a rash was breaking out all over her neck. Snatching up a damp cloth, she swirled it in her bowl of cool water, turned her back on him while she cleaned off the mess in front of her little mirror on the table. 'It's not mud. It's my chocolate and avocado mask.'

With her face cleansed of its rich goo, her skin naked and baby-soft, she turned back—reluctantly—to find he'd closed the distance between them. She leaned back, held up her palms. 'Too close. I'm not wear—'

'You're stunning without make-up.'

'I wasn't angling for a compliment.'

'It's not a compliment, it's a fact.'

The wonder of his gruff words filled her with light; she felt the glow to the soles of her feet. 'I'm no make-up model but thank you anyway.'

But he was still seeing her at a disadvantage. To get even, she dipped a finger in the chocolate concoction. 'How would you look with a moustache?' She smeared it slowly just above his upper lip. 'Made from all natural products. Cocoa powder, avocado, coconut milk and oil.

'More?' she asked, when he didn't move, just watched her as if he were made of stone. Leo Hamilton was no Sensitive New Age Guy. 'Relax,' she soothed. 'Ever been out with a beauty therapist?' She smeared another dollop on his chin, rubbing in a gentle circular motion, enjoying the feel of masculine stubble beneath her fingertips.

'No.'

She smiled at his mouth. 'You have the most irresistible cupid's bow I've ever seen on a man.'

She reached out a finger but he grasped her hand and held it away. 'I've been fantasising about kissing you again all week.'

Their eyes clashed, silver on black. 'I know,' she murmured.

Her pulse leapt as he slid his lips over hers. Once. Twice. Brushing back and forth in that unhurried way he had that she was fast learning to savour and appreciate.

Only their lips touched. His were rich and firm and promised pleasures yet to be explored and enjoyed. Pure pleasure. Physical enjoyment, nothing more, she told herself.

But it felt like a lot more and her body shivered though the afternoon sun shone warm on her skin. The fragrance of his freshly soaped skin mingled with the surrounding scents of basil and thyme and lemon verbena.

Then he nibbled on her lower lip with his teeth, so lightly she wanted to cry with the bewildering gentleness. She tipped her head back, arched her neck, silently pleading for more, but Leo wouldn't be drawn. Not yet.

'*How* do you know?' he muttered against her mouth.

'I just know.' She also knew men like Leo—powerful men supremely confident in their sexual magnetism and charm—wouldn't be entirely reassured by that cryptic wise-woman answer.

She tilted her head so that she could see his fine masculine features properly. 'I've been fantasising about you too.'

'I know.' His mouth twitched with humour.

She reached out to touch the full bottom lip. 'Why wouldn't I? I'm a healthy single woman and you're a single, attractive man. Right?'

He dipped a finger in her bowl of chocolate, dabbed a smudge on her chin, then licked it off with one unhurried swipe of his tongue.

Her eyes drifted to half-mast as her body ached in an unfamiliar way. He was good. Slow was good, slow was—

'You could use some sweetener.'

Her eyes snapped open and she snorted at his grimace of distaste. 'It's not meant to be body paint.'

His eyes sharpened, the glint of a sword in sunlight, tempting her with its promise of silvery delight.

'But it could be,' she suggested, silkily. 'Some other time.'

'When?'

She smiled her best seductive woman's smile at the sexual need in his voice and ran a finger from his Adam's apple to the bottom stud on his expensive leather jacket, lingering tantalisingly above the growing bulge in his jeans. 'I'll let you know.'

But before she could step away, he dragged her against him with both hands, the promise in those sharp eyes morphing to impatience. His own reactive emotion obviously annoyed him. 'I don't respond well to being manipulated, Breanna.'

Biting back a grin, she blinked up at him. 'Is that what you think I'm doing?'

His hands shifted from her arms to her spine to her bottom, where he crushed her against his body. 'You know exactly what you're doing.'

The hot, rigid length of him pressed against her and she let him know with a tiny subtle shift of her hips just how much she was enjoying it. 'I'm not manipulating you.' Smiling, she met his eyes and her hands hovered at the waistband of his jeans. 'Yet.'

His nostrils flared, his jaw tightened, those eyes smouldering silver with honest-to-goodness lust. Warning her not to start something she didn't intend to finish.

'When I do,' she continued confidently, 'you'll know about i—'

His mouth swooped on hers, snatching the rest of her words. Dominating, demanding, determined. She felt that tight leash of his slip a notch, as, with ruthless insistence, his tongue forced her lips apart and dived inside to duel with hers.

Heat sizzled along her lips, her veins, while images whirled through her mind. The two of them right there on the uneven bricks finishing this.

And even though she felt the urgency humming through him, through them both, even though he didn't relinquish his tight grip on her bottom, he gentled his kiss, settled in. And, oh…the sweet, seductive flavour of him. His need hot, matching her own.

Leo was having a hard time staying upright as soft feminine hands tugged at the hem of his shirt and slipped beneath. His stomach muscles contracted violently. He hadn't intended to kiss her; he'd wanted to teach her a lesson in… he couldn't remember what…and now—hell—he was in all kinds of bother.

Somehow, he pried his lips from hers long enough to drag in air and relinquish his hold on her jersey-covered butt. She gazed up at him, cheeks flushed with desire, mouth damp and wide and wicked. He swore silently and hoped she hadn't noticed his restraint was ready to snap.

Her fingernails scraped over his nipples, sending darts of lust twanging through his body. His breath hissed out and he shuddered, capturing and restraining her hands.

Brie thanked her stars he'd had the willpower she seemed to be lacking. It made it marginally easier to pull her hands out of his grip and step back and…*breathe, Brie.*

How could she have got so carried away? It was just a kiss. *Just a kiss.* And she had a zillion things to do. On the top of her list was organising West Wind for her new tenant. 'No body painting today.' Forcing casualness into her voice, she inhaled a long breath while she waited for her pulse to slow. 'Or tonight. I have a previous engagement.'

The frank transparency of lust faded from his eyes as he stuffed the front of his shirt back into his waistband. He glanced at her make-up stash on the table. 'A previous engagement?'

She glared at him, annoyed at the ridiculous question she saw in his gaze. Annoyed that he obviously assumed tonight's engagement was a party. She could clarify, but *why should she when he was ready to assume the worst*?

'I would *not* have kissed you if I was dating another man tonight, let's get that clear.' She should *not* have to explain herself. Not to him, not to anyone. She turned away and began stacking her pots back into plastic containers, glad she had something to do. More than annoyance, his doubts and assumptions tore at a vulnerable place inside her. The place Elliot had helped sculpt, the place she'd taught herself not to acknowledge.

The place she reminded herself now that did not exist.

'That didn't come out the way it was meant to.'

'Is that an apology?' She waved a hand in his general direction as she packed then thought better of it. 'Forget I said that and we'll call it even.'

A few heavy seconds passed, then he asked, 'Are we good?'

'We're good.' Picking up her box, she headed for the back door, leaving him to follow. At the door she turned to him. 'Really. We're good.' She smiled, impatient to demonstrate he couldn't get to her emotionally but not quite able to meet those eyes. 'I apologise that the house is still a mess. I'll get right on it.'

'I can see if there's a room available in town for this evening.'

'*No.*' Plonking her box on the kitchen table, she heaved an inward sigh at the mess in front of her. 'You *will* have a place to sleep here tonight.' Somewhere.

'In that case, I've got a few errands in the city. I'll need a key if you're going out before I get back.'

'The spare's on the hook next to your fire blanket if you want to take it now.' She gestured to it while she cleared the table and loaded the dishwasher.

The moment he left, she slammed the dishwasher shut, grabbed water and detergent and set to work with a scrubbing brush.

Annoyance turned to severe aggravation, made worse by his lingering scent in her nostrils, which in turn lent her speed and energy as she moved like a dervish through the kitchen chores. He assumed too much and too frequently and so far his assumptions had been unreasonable and way off the mark. Her house party and sick guest confrontation for starters. She also had a gut feeling he'd turned up at her party last Saturday in the first instance because he'd *assumed* they were boozy affairs and wanted to check. Yep, that would fit his personality profile.

She loved to party and she loved to flirt and did so regularly and often. But when friends or others, even people she didn't know, needed her help or support, as with Megan and her migraine, there was never any question— they were her priority.

Hands fisted on hips, she scanned her kitchen, rarely tidy, now sparkling like new beneath the down-lights. Ready for Mr Hamilton to use—if he ever cooked. He probably had a personal chef-cum-housekeeper.

They had this extraordinary attraction thing going on but, away from the fantasy world they seemed to be playing in, who was Leo Hamilton? She did know he was quick to criticise. Ready to assume the bad. She dusted off her hands. So for tonight, let him assume.

Staying out of Breanna's way was the wisest course so Leo didn't return until seven o'clock. In case she hadn't had time to eat, he'd bought her a pizza when he'd bought his own.

He needn't have bothered because she was long gone. He found a note addressed to him on the kitchen table.

Leo, I've made up a bed in the bedroom at the far end of the passage. Apologies, the bed's a bit small but it's only for tonight. B
PS Don't wait up xx

Kisses from the girl who'd put him in the bedroom furthest from hers?

He wanted more than paper kisses. A lot more. He'd never met a woman who intrigued him so. Then again, he'd never met a woman quite like Breanna. No, that wasn't entirely true. He'd met those confident, liberated women, but had avoided getting tangled up with any of them. After the sex went stale, what did they have in common? They were too independent, too confrontational.

Too much trouble all round.

So why was he walking through her house, having struck a deal with her, and checking out the rooms they'd agreed he could use—including her bedroom with the only bed big enough to accommodate his height?

En route he saw a couple of suitcases and cardboard boxes stashed by the front door ready for her to take with her to her brother's retreat tomorrow. Great, he told himself. Out of his way. Out of temptation's way.

Every one of those pre-agreed-on rooms was tidy, with the exception of her bedroom, which was still in the throes of a battle not yet won. Because he didn't think he could sleep comfortably beneath rose florals and flounces, he'd purchased a Lincoln green quilt cover and plump feather pillow for his stay. But for tonight they'd be sleeping under the same roof, a few short steps apart.

Five hours later, he was stretched out on the sofa in the living room and asking himself why he was still awake and wondering what time party princesses came home. Or if they came home…

Breanna had been adamant she was going solo this evening, insulted that he'd suggested otherwise, but what if she'd met someone tonight? The thought bothered him more than it should. And *that* bothered him. Because what self-respecting man would choose to hook up with a woman as temperamental and stubbornly independent as Breanna Black?

He heard her car pull up and realised his appearance downstairs would suggest he'd been doing what she'd told him not to do: waiting up for her. He remained where he was because he didn't respond to demands; furthermore, to retreat now would only make him appear guilty of same.

His first glimpse of her in a sexy black dress had him wanting to sit up straighter and take notice. Of every dip and every curve, the long, lean, toned muscles in her legs and arms as she tossed a long-haired black and maroon jacket onto the sofa.

'You're still up.' Her bag followed the jacket down.

He shifted his inspection to her face and noticed dark smudges beneath her eyes. Socialising too hard and too often could do that. His cynicism or personal experience? 'I'm never in bed till one.' Unless…

'So you weren't waiting up for me.'

'No.'

'That's a relief, 'cos I'm stuffed.' Crossing the room, she collapsed onto the armchair opposite him and yawned. 'So, do you go to bed late by choice, or do you work late hours?'

'Both.'

'When I get the chance, I like to curl up at seven and sleep for twelve hours.' She kicked off her black patent stilettos, closed her eyes and murmured, 'Unfortunately, the opportunity doesn't occur very often.'

It was her choice to party, but she looked somehow vulnerable with her black lashes resting on paler than usual cheeks. He'd bet she didn't make a habit of allowing that aspect to reveal itself. He almost felt sorry for her and volunteered, 'I could have picked you up,' before he could censor himself.

'Whatever for?' Her eyes snapped open. 'Let's be clear here. I enjoy spending time in a man's company. I enjoy it a lot and I enjoy it often. How I choose to spend that time depends on the man, the timing.' She flipped a hand. 'Even the weather. Point being, I like men but I don't need one to look after me.'

Fascinating. Leo hadn't noticed until this moment how irritation caused the outer corner of her left eye to twitch and how both eyes glinted with tiny speckles of gold in the Tiffany lamp light on the table beside her. How the more fiery she became, the fuller, and more tempting, her bottom lip appeared to be.

'You conduct your sexual activities according to the weather?'

'Whatever.' Her eyes slid closed once more and Leo could almost see the feistiness drain away. 'I need to sleep,' she murmured.

That much was obvious. 'Do I offer to sweep you into my arms and upstairs?'

'Not necessary. Nor do I need tucking in—in case you were wondering.' She rallied enough to lever herself off the chair, grab her bag and stumble her way barefoot to the foyer. 'Breakfast's on you,' she said, over her shoulder. 'Night.'

'Goodnight.'

He heard her door close and imagined her falling face down on her bed, maybe slipping off her dress first…

Like unwelcome guests, those provocative images refused to leave. Lust licked through him, hot and restless
and unassuaged. So he strolled to her bookcase to check
out her taste in reading material. Flicked through a couple of classics, a biography of Amelia Earhart. He discovered an entire shelf of first editions in pristine condition
behind glass and was settling down with Stephen King's
Carrie when he heard a jingle coming from inside Breanna's jacket.

He considered answering it but what would be the point?
When the second call came two minutes later, he was curious enough to take her phone from the inside pocket and
check caller ID. Sam. No surname, no photo. No telling if
Sam was male or female. And none of his business.

On the third call, because there was a possibility of
some kind of emergency, he answered. 'Breanna Black's
phone. Leo Hamilton speaking.'

'Oh.' The female voice sounded flustered, as if she
might be catching Breanna at a sensitive or inopportune
moment. 'Is Brie…is Brie there? Are you…?'

'Her new tenant,' he clarified before the woman could
jump to the wrong conclusion. 'Did she mention renting
her house out for a short while?'

'She did. You're the guy from the party last weekend,
right?'

'Yeah. And you're…?' He tried to recall meeting a
woman called Sam.

'You were looking for a couple of glasses?'

'Ah, *Samantha*.' The redhead. 'Brie's gone to bed. She
left her phone downstairs. Can I help?'

'You certainly can. If Brie hasn't mentioned her purse
is missing then she hasn't noticed yet but she dropped it on
the footpath outside her salon tonight. We share the same
professional rooms—I'm a remedial massage therapist and
we had a session here this evening. Can you tell her I've

put it in our safe? That way she can come by and collect it when she wakes up.'

Breanna hadn't mentioned her salon this afternoon. Her face had been covered in goo while she massaged her feet with some sweet-smelling concoction—her focus on partying and looking good while she did so. 'I'll let her know.' He was about to disconnect but Sam got in first.

'Great, thanks. Hopefully she'll get a decent sleep. On top of cleaning up the house for you, she's worked her butt off this past week.' Sam sounded as if she considered it entirely his fault that Breanna had left the place in a mess until the last possible moment.

'If I don't see her, I'll leave her a note.' He sat down then stretched out on the sofa, letting his fingers run through the strands of Breanna's long-haired jacket. 'So, she was working tonight?'

'Yes. She looked done in when she got here but she refused to postpone because she didn't want to let them down.'

Leo frowned. Hadn't she been going to a party? Glamming up for an evening on the town?

Not according to Sam.

Yet she hadn't challenged his party princess gibe. Further, she'd accepted full responsibility for her lack of organisation and the whole forgotten schedule business without saying a *damn thing* in her defence. What had happened to the straight-talking Breanna? And who were the mysterious *them* she hadn't wanted to let down? 'You said a session. What do you mean by that?'

'Brie's been working with cancer survivors on a monthly basis,' Sam explained. 'Demonstrating how to care for their skin after chemo and radiation and using her home-made natural products, which she experiments with in her spare time. And that's on top of salon hours, which includes taking on extra patients who can't afford to pay.' Sam ended her glowing testament with, 'She's one of a kind.'

In other words, *Brie's more than you think.* 'Thanks for letting me know,' he said. 'I'll make sure she hears she's appreciated.'

He disconnected, his legs hanging over one end of the sofa while he caressed Breanna's jacket some more. He'd have been none the wiser if Sam hadn't filled him in. There was much more to Breanna than he'd first thought. And he meant what he'd said—he intended letting her know.

CHAPTER SIX

LEO SET UP Breanna's dining room as his temporary office. He'd been up since the crack of dawn, due in part to the cramped bed he'd been assigned but mostly because he had a business commitment this evening and he wanted to ensure everything was organised before taking Breanna out to breakfast and seeing what other activities she'd planned for today.

She might spend the early part of the afternoon with him before he left for his three-hour drive to Heaven. He was due to dine with the owners and developers of the east coast's luxury eco-lodge this evening.

He wanted to make up for yesterday's badly timed visit. He wanted to know why a straight-talking woman like Breanna hadn't set him straight about her evening's plans. Most of all, he wanted a little more up close and personal time with her.

Earlier, he'd brought in a load of groceries and made room for them in a kitchen cupboard. He'd made himself space on a refrigerator shelf until Breanna took what she wanted when she left. He didn't need much; he rarely cooked. He'd left his new pillow and quilt on the tiny half-bed he'd slept in last night before taking a brisk walk in the early morning chill followed by an almost as chilly shower.

Over a quick breakfast of instant coffee he found hiding at the back of the cupboard and thick, buttered toast,

he logged on to the internet and did some banking trans-
actions. He went over his report for this evening, made
a couple of last-minute changes. By the time he phoned
Sunny she was having brunch with friends in one of Melbourne's trendy arcades and shopping was on her afternoon
agenda. Seemed nothing slowed his sister down.

He made a couple more calls, then surfed the net for
relevant articles on current environmental trends while he
waited for Breanna to wake.

At ten-fifteen, he was onto his second coffee when he
heard movement upstairs, then the splash of Breanna's
shower. His skin started to itch. He rubbed at the back
of his neck and stared at his laptop's screen. He tried to
concentrate on the words but the cascading sound from
above made him think of shower sex. Of sweet-smelling
soap and slippery rose-petal skin. Of how long it had been
since he'd indulged in that particular activity.

Which had him wondering: when had he stopped thinking of Breanna as Sunny's neighbourly support person and
started thinking of her as his next lover? The thought un-
settled Leo as much now as it had that first time he'd laid
eyes on her and he itched in a way he'd never itched before.

He itched some more when Breanna appeared beneath
the dining-room arch smelling fresh and looking fabulous
in indigo-blue jeans and a tight navy sweater that showcased her assets to full advantage. She wore her jeans
tucked into caramel-coloured calf-length boots and her
hair swung free about her face. Stunning.

She saw him watching—ogling—and smiled. 'Good
morning.'

It was a good morning now. She was like the sun rising
on a beautiful day. 'Morning.' He cleared a sudden husk
from his throat and asked, 'How did you sleep?'

She shook out an orange scarf covered in little black

owls. 'Very well. I suppose the same can't be said for you? I'm sorry about the bed.'

'You could have offered to share yours.'

Her grin was quick and lively. 'Is breakfast still on?'

'You bet.'

'Great, I'm starved.' She wound the scarf around her neck, slung her bag on her shoulder. 'Shall we go? Or are you busy?' She tagged the last on as an afterthought.

For her, this morning, he was prepared to drop everything and go just to be with her. 'I'm free until later this afternoon.'

'In that case I've changed my mind about breakfast. There's a new wine and cheese place in Richmond having an open day today on their lawns. The weather's going to be fine, it's only a half-hour's drive and I've been dying to try it.'

She switched from one idea to the next so fast she made his head spin. He was learning she only had one speed: fast forward. 'Wine on an empty stomach?'

'Today's my first day off in two weeks. I've got twenty-one hours left before I have to go back to work and I don't want to waste it.'

'It's a date, then.'

'Nuh-uh. Not a date.' She shook her head but her eyes danced. 'Sunday sessions don't count as dates, especially in the morning.'

'Okay, it's a non-date.'

He watched her cross the room to fetch last night's jacket, which was still on the sofa, then she caught sight of her phone on the coffee table and frowned. Looked straight at him with accusing eyes.

'Samantha rang last night,' he informed her.

'You answered my phone?'

'When it rang three times in succession, I figured it might be important. I was right. You dropped your purse outside your salon. Sam said to let you know she put it in the safe.'

'Really? Jeez….' Her expression turned appreciative. 'Thanks. I hadn't even noticed…what is wrong with me lately?' Her shoulders lifted and she rolled her eyes at the ceiling.

'Coffee—or whatever it is you drink—before we go? You look like you need it. I'll make it—I was going to make another coffee for myself anyway.'

'Okay. Thanks. Green tea. Red tin with yellow cows, on the shelf above the kettle.'

Brie followed him into the kitchen, sat down and took in the view as he reached for the tin. She was going to have to keep her hands from straying to that soft mohair jumper he was wearing that matched his eyes perfectly. And those sexy-as-sin jeans.

'Do you cook?'

'Not if I can help it.' He set a steaming cup in front of her then set the sugar and the carton of milk on the table between them. Finally, with his own mug, he slid into the chair opposite.

'Join the club—I'm no cook either.' She laughed. 'We'd be no good as housemates.'

He poured in milk then cradled his mug between his hands. Steely eyes studied her. 'Why didn't you tell me about last night?'

So Sam had blabbed. Brie wondered how much. She raised the tea to her lips, took a long, slow sip—soothing and fragrant—and said, 'What about last night?'

'Sam told me, so don't pretend you don't know what I'm talking about.'

'I know exactly what you're talking about.' She smiled at him over the rim of her mug, knowing he'd expected a different answer. 'As for why I didn't tell you, I'll let you figure it out for yourself, Leo.'

Jaw rigid, he stared at her for a long minute, his eyes turning a darker shade of grey. He gulped down the rest of his drink, set his mug down with a clunk of china on wood and leaned back in his chair.

He really didn't get it, she decided, and drained the last of her tea. It wouldn't occur to him that Leo Hamilton, obvious chick magnet, might draw a wrong conclusion when it came to women. And she wasn't going to enlighten him. She pushed up from the table and rinsed her mug, set it on the drainer. 'Okay, while you're thinking about it, let's make a start before it rains.'

'Didn't you say the weather's going to be fine today?'

'It's four seasons in one day here—you'll be used to that, coming from Melbourne.' She shrugged into her jacket. 'I have to pick up my purse before we head out of town. Are you driving or will I?'

'Is that a serious question?'

'Why wouldn't it be?' She searched her pockets for gloves, stuffed them in her bag. 'It makes sense; I'm local and—'

'It's not a problem,' he interrupted, swiping up his leather jacket and producing a set of keys from the pocket. 'I might not be local but I do know my way around Tasmania's main roads. We'll take your luggage as well, get it out of the way.'

'We'll do that later,' she said, refusing to let him have it all his way. 'We don't have time now. Brunch beckons.'

Fortunately he didn't argue or it might have got nasty. She climbed into his car and they drove the five minutes to Eve's Naturally. Even in his spacious vehicle it felt too close, too intimate. Breathing in his scent. Aware of his long tanned fingers on the steering wheel. The way her

body seemed to lean towards his a little too much whenever they took a left turn. And even when they didn't.

'I only meant we need more time at the retreat because
I want to show you what the Pink Snowflake's been able
to achieve.'

'No worries, so long as we're there before three.' He
negotiated around a bus. 'I have a dinner meeting at six
this evening but it's a three hour drive if I stick to the
speed limit.'

'Which you will, of course.'

'Of course.'

'So you'll be staying there overnight, then?'

'Yes.'

'And this client needs your environmental management
consulting expertise?' She checked out his strong, masculine jaw in profile. 'Did I get it right?'

'Yes and yes.'

'So where are you going that takes three hours?'

'Heaven.'

She laughed. But she didn't laugh so much as sigh at
the way he glanced at her after he said it. As if... 'Say a
prayer for me when you get there.'

She watched his lips curve but he kept his eyes on the
road as he asked, 'Have you ever been?'

'To heaven? Yeah, I've been. But you're talking about
the resort. Not at those unaffordable prices.' She indicated
Eve's Naturally amongst a row of spacious offices on the
left. 'You can stop here. I'll be two secs.'

Then they were on their way out of suburbia, headed towards the historic town of Richmond with its charming
little cottages and her favourite old-fashioned English
sweet shop.

Brie kept up a running commentary, pointing out local
places of interest, telling him what she knew about the Blue

Bandicoot winery they were going to be visiting, which they would reach before the town of Richmond itself.

Leo checked his speed as Breanna chatted on about the passing scenery and the area's history. Her tour-guide conversation kept his mind from straying to impure thoughts about how they might turn off onto one of the narrow side roads, pull over, recline the seats and engage in creative and mutually satisfying sex.

The more he tried to concentrate on her words, the more vivid and creative his imagination grew and the stronger the ache in his groin became. His gaze slid sideways. She was looking out of the side window, giving him a view of her neck, pale and creamy and exposed as she talked. He forced his eyes straight ahead and tried to concentrate on the road.

'Am I boring you?' The sharp tone of her voice a moment later pierced his lusty thoughts.

'What? No. Of course not. I've driven on this road before but I can say, in all honesty, it's never been such an interesting journey.'

She snorted. 'You don't say.'

'I do say.'

'Nuh-uh.' He heard her shift sideways in her seat to look at him. 'What were you *really* thinking, Leo? While I was telling you about the history of the winery?'

'If I told you, we'd have to take a detour and stop for a bit and I don't have time today.'

The car filled with a wordless anticipation. 'Forget the wine and cheese,' she said slowly. 'Brunch is overrated.'

He ignored her sensual tone that slid through his lower belly like a hot knife. 'I've been up since six and I'm hungry. Enough of the tour-guide talk, tell me about you.'

'How about what I'd like to do to you right now?' She sucked in a breath between her teeth. 'Or what I'd like you to do to me?'

'We both know it's a bad idea to pursue that particular conversation while I'm driving. Something less...vivid.'

'Oka-ay. So when my father died six years ago, I discovered I have a half-brother. It took me three years to track Jett down in Paris, so I was technically an only child growing up. And now he's just married my best friend, so—'

'*You*, not your brother. Tell me about *you*.'

'I love vanilla ice cream drenched in hot chocolate sauce.'

'Do y—?'

'I love the contrasts of hot and cold on my nipples. And I especially love it when someone—'

'Stop. You're deliberately provoking me.' And he was responding exactly the way she wanted him to. *Not going to happen, Breanna.* He tightened his hands on the wheel.

'Provoking you? Mmm, I hope so,' she murmured, and he could almost feel the trail of her fingernail down his upper arm even though he knew her not-so-innocent hands lay innocently in her lap. 'You could pull over...and...'

'We could, but I'm hungry.' A tingling sensation akin to pins and needles danced down his left arm and into his fingers.

Heat, desire and an altogether different kind of hunger was building within the car like a tropical thunderstorm. He switched off the heater, flicked open the upper air vent and tugged at the neck of his jumper. He didn't find overconfident women a turn-on; why was his body responding so carnally to this one?

'According to the GPS, the turn-off to the winery's in one kilometre,' she said. From the corner of his eye he saw her stretch her arms over her head. 'Your last chance.'

'Or what?' Checking the rear-view mirror, he pulled to the side of the road, tyres skidding on the gravel as he brought the vehicle to a fast stop. He tossed his sunglasses on the dash, unclipped his seat belt and leaned over so that their faces were centimetres apart. He could still smell her shower scent, the subtle fragrance of her make-up. 'Are you saying there won't be another?'

She took off her sunglasses too, drew a circle on his thigh with a fingertip, looked at him from beneath sooty lashes. 'I'm not saying that at all. I meant last chance before lunch—or brunch. Whatever. So kiss me.' Her demand came out more like a needy plea.

Better, he thought, watching her pupils dilate, her glossy lips part slightly in expectation. 'You're not interested in exercising your feminist proclivities and kissing me first?'

She wiggled closer on her seat, fingers spreading warmth over his thigh, breasts tantalisingly close to his chest but not quite touching. *Tempt and tease.* 'I liked how you kissed me yesterday and I want you to kiss me again.'

His gaze dropped to her mouth, yesterday's spicy memory, today a sweet anticipation. 'Then we can go and eat?'

'If that's all you want from me.'

To his surprise, her direct gaze changed, became almost vulnerable. As if deep down she feared rejection and had made a lifetime of proving she didn't. 'Not even close,' he murmured, taking her face between his hands and laying his lips on hers.

But there was nothing hesitant about the way she kissed him back. Her kiss was as warm and full-flavoured as he remembered, her competent therapist's fingers firm as she slid them around his neck and into his hair.

He didn't know how long their lips remained locked together. Didn't much care. He was still determining how far to take this here on the side of a reasonably busy road when she made the decision for him, pulling away with a breathless, 'Whoa. We're forgetting we're in public here.' Her cheeks were flushed; her eyes still held that hint of lost kitten.

'I hadn't forgotten.' Surprised, he raised his brows. 'That bothers you?'

'No. Yes. We should get going.'

With a finger on her chin, he tilted her face to his before she could scrabble to put her sunglasses back on. Her tempt and tease routine was a façade. She was maintaining an emotional distance, if not a physical one. Which was more than fine with him. Still, he wondered what had spooked her. He shifted back behind the wheel, slid his own sunglasses back on. 'Let's go find something to eat.'

The wine estate was a celebration of colour, sound and flavours. Even though the vines had been pruned and tied in preparation for spring growth, the sky was blue, the last autumnal foliage still clung to deciduous trees, giving the atmosphere a glorious golden hue despite the chill in the air. A jazz band played in the barn area of the vineyard's historic stables, wine sparkled, the aroma of cheese mingled with fried onions from the nearby barbecue.

Despite the undercurrent of low-grade sparks that sizzled between them, Leo found Brie's wit and humour complemented his own as they worked their way through a variety of wines and cheeses and the inevitable sausage sizzle. True to typical Tasmanian tradition, the clouds eventually rolled in and the party turned soggy. They shared his umbrella on the way back to the car while she fed him pieces of quince-paste-lathered cracker.

As a responsible and sober driver, he drove them back, allowing plenty of time for Breanna to show him the McPherson retreat, named after a generous benefactor. But Breanna was dozing ten minutes after leaving the winery, catching up on her lack of sleep. He ought to be relieved, but, oddly, it was disappointment that dragged at him for the rain-soaked drive back to Hobart.

* * *

When Brie pried heavy eyes half open, she was looking at the familiar high-walled gate of the retreat through Leo's rain-washed windscreen. His voice was low, his warm breath tickling her cheek. She couldn't make out what he was saying but she wanted to slide back into sleep with that sexy murmur against her ear.

'Wake up, baby doll.' Sharper this time.

She blinked at the ridiculously incongruous term as it applied to her and snorted, 'That's a first.' She pushed up, annoyed that she'd dozed off in front of Leo. More annoyed that he'd woken her from such exciting dreams.

'Security code.' He sounded vaguely impatient, as if he'd asked her a few times already.

She recited it to him, then forced some energy into her voice and said, 'I need my stuff. And my car.'

'All taken care of.' The gates slid back and he drove through. 'Your stuff's in the back but you won't be driving for a few hours yet after that alcohol. I'll drop you back at your house on my way to the coast if you want to stay there tonight and drive here tomorrow.'

He'd stopped and loaded her gear and she hadn't woken? How was that possible? Maybe it had something to do with how super-relaxed she was feeling with the wine's pleasant warmth still buzzing through her system. 'Thanks, anyway, but I'll be staying here tonight. And thanks for loading my stuff. I appreciate it. I'll catch a cab to work tomorrow morning—I can pick the car up later.' She'd been hanging out for her regular soak in the retreat's spa all week and nothing was going to keep her from it.

She climbed out and the ground beneath her feet tilted a bit. 'Come on in,' she said, digging out her keys.

She pushed open the front door, smiled and breathed deep as the fresh smell of new work met her nostrils. 'I'll be moving Eve's Naturally here as soon as Jett and Olivia return. I can't wait to be a part of Livvy's exciting vision.'

'You sound as if you're trying to sell it.'

'It sells itself. And even better, we're able to offer subsidised rates to disadvantaged clients, thanks to generous ongoing donations through Pink Snowflake—which your valuable and generous rent is going to.'

They spent a few minutes unloading her gear before she showed him around. She was so proud to be able to talk up and show off the professional services in addition to personal fitness coaches, the range of areas from solarium to meditation and yoga plus a fully staffed kitchen specialising in organic food. She pointed out the gorgeous bushland and river views visible from floor-to-ceiling windows.

'It's going to open for business as soon as the happy couple can drag themselves back from honeymoon-land,' she told him, switching on the heating and shrugging out of her jacket. 'It'll be a couple of months yet but we already have clients booked in.'

'I can believe it.' Leo wasn't easily excited about the projects he saw on a daily basis but this unique set-up was something else. The creative use of space. The sparkling fixtures, recessed lighting, marble and honeyed Tasmanian Oak. The relaxing use of muted colours: mulberry and charcoal, blue and cream. The way it harmonised with the surrounding environment.

And the foundation that had made it possible.

He held a growing respect for these guys who'd pulled it together. 'I'm impressed. And I don't say that often.'

'Of course you are, and I'm sure you don't, Mr Hamilton.' There was a smile in her voice as she tugged off her boots and nodded to another wing they'd not yet explored. 'Take off your shoes then come and see my favourite place to relax in.'

He did, and moments later he saw an indoor pool with a blue and grey and green vista stretching all the way to the coast. Today the view was misty and waterlogged with rain sluicing down the huge panes. 'I see why you love it.'

'We're not quite there yet,' she said with a glint in her eyes and moved towards an archway on the far side.

He followed her to a massive shiny white spa surrounded by marble and gold and enclosed in glass. The same panorama of flora and river spread out before them.

Privacy with a view.

'But if you want a change in scenery...' Breanna pressed a remote.

Panels slid down on silent tracks, blocking all light and sound from the outside and leaving them bathed in a soft blush. Leo noted vaguely that the architect had designed a curvature in the panels, which prevented the light from the pool filtering into the spa's area. The rest of the world ceased to exist as the watery sound of a harp trickled like silver over imaginary moss. The stresses of the last few days slid away. Afternoon turned to hot summer night as the floor beneath his bare feet warmed and he drank in the sight of Brie surrounded by a pink aura.

Her close-fitting dark clothes showcased her long limbs and slender body, her rounded breasts and mysterious eyes. It was almost as if he were under a spell.

And he might have spoken to tell her how amazing she looked, how much he wanted her and damn the consequences, but to speak would somehow seem irreverent at that moment.

He heard the sound of bare feet on marble as she crossed the room and lit half a dozen fat candles. The scent of sandalwood soon drifted on the air and he breathed slow and deep. It was almost as if she was seducing him.

Except she'd done nothing overtly provocative, nothing to entice him to play her game. Whatever her game was.

Should have heeded that glint in her eyes earlier.

Shaking himself out of the fog that enshrouded him, he concentrated on opening and closing his fists. Taking short sharp breaths.

What time was it? He checked his watch, swore under his breath. With the weather the way it was, he'd take longer to get to the coast than he'd planned. 'I have to go.' He flicked an impatient hand at the walls. 'If you'd remove the privacy screens, please.'

'Are you sure I can't tempt you to stay a little longer?' But even as she spoke the panels slid away and the intimate mood vanished, replaced by the cool glare of a wet afternoon.

'It's a—'

'Three-hour drive,' she finished for him. 'I know.' They turned and retraced their steps to where they'd left their shoes.

He put his on then straightened to look at her. Barefoot, her hair tousled from her earlier car nap and the inclement weather. Again, as it had earlier, her expression tugged at something inside him but he dismissed it in the same heartbeat. 'Catch you later.'

'If you change your mind, or decide to come back early…' She stared up at him, eyes deep and dark and perceptive. 'You'll remember the code to get through the gate,' she said, reaching into her jeans pocket. 'And here's a keycard for the retreat. You might want to use it sometime.'

'I won't need it,' he told her, but found himself taking it anyway. It was warm from its proximity to her skin. An invitation he *would* resist.

'That's entirely up to you.' She walked to the door, opened it. A gust of wet wind blew in with a flurry of leaves. She shivered and folded her arms tight across her shoulders. 'Glad I'm going to be warm and cosy here.'

'I'm glad you are too,' he said. 'Have a pleasant evening.' And, turning before he could change his mind, he dashed through the downpour to his car.

There was no way he was going to be late for this meeting. No way in heaven.

CHAPTER SEVEN

WHO WAS BRIE? Leo pondered the riddle as he negotiated Hobart's Derwent Bridge in heavy rain. The playful tease or the little girl lost? The up-front woman who insisted on honesty or the compassionate campaigner he'd only glimpsed beneath that flirty exterior—a side he'd not known existed until his conversation with Sam.

Obviously she didn't do deep and meaningful relationships. And wasn't that what he wanted too? A hot and mutually satisfying no-nonsense fling with no drama when one or both of them called it quits and moved on?

Assuming he wanted a fling with a woman who liked to be in the driver's seat.

Thoughts of driving prompted him to check the time again. In this weather he was going to be later than planned. He'd call ahead when he was out of the suburbs and let them know the state of the roads and his ETA.

His thoughts turned relentlessly to Breanna again. *Did* he want a fling with a woman who called it as she saw it? A stunning and sexy woman who wasn't afraid to let him know what she wanted? He found her personality surprisingly stimulating and refreshingly different. He found their subtle power tussles a challenge.

Leo thrived on challenge.

She'd all but seduced him earlier; he still didn't know how she'd managed it without a touch, without one flirtatious word. Just that on-again off-again wicked glint in her eyes. So she wanted to play? He saw a U-turn opening in the road up ahead and flicked on his indicator.

Game on.

And he *would* win.

Brie was waiting for him on wide-cushioned matting at the edge of the spa when she saw his car pull up on the security monitor. Smiling, she rubbed her hands together in satisfaction—and spine-tingling expectation. She'd known he'd come back. She knew men. If there was a choice between a new lover and work they chose the sex every time. Leo Hamilton was no different.

So after he'd left this afternoon, she'd lowered the panels again. The light was a dim blush once more. She'd cranked up the temperature in the air and in the spa, changed the music to mellow blues and added a couple of essential oil burners to the candlelight for a soothing and relaxing atmosphere. She'd turned dismal day into sultry night.

A quick make-up repair then she'd changed into a long silk garment of midnight blue, leaving her feet bare. She'd wavered between sexy underwear or none at all, and had decided to initiate her new tangerine lace with black trim, which had cost her almost a week's takings. She hoped he appreciated it before she let him take it off her. Because it was all about the sex and what man didn't enjoy a little mystery to unwrap first?

And it was going to be good. Better than good. Because they understood each other from the start. He wasn't her type, she wasn't his but they had this *thing* going on. It would be casual, fun sex. Temporary. Something to enjoy and work out of their systems then move on. *No heart, no hurt.*

Suddenly there he was. Before she was quite ready for him. A darker silhouette against the dark panels. Only his eyes flashed in the wavering candlelight. Power emanated from that gaze. Strength. Control. Dominance.

And for the first time in her life with a new lover, she felt a flicker of nerves zip down her body.

Not fear. She knew on an instinctive level he'd never harm her. This was something deeper, something primal. Something that tore her open and left her defenceless. And a growing awareness that here was the potential for pain of a different kind. If she let there be..

'Come here, Breanna.' Calmly spoken, his demand bounced off the walls and vibrated through her body as he tossed his jacket down.

'It's more comfortable here,' she began. 'There's—'

'*Now*, Breanna.' All semblance of calm vanished, impatience rolled in like thunder to take its place. 'And bring that remote with you, wherever it is.'

She picked it up from the low table as she walked—in a deliberately relaxed fashion—towards him. *Relaxed?* Her insides were quivering, her knees liquefying.

His hand shot out, palm up. She met his gaze force for force as she handed him the remote. Up close he looked even more formidable. Almost the way he'd looked the first time she'd seen him. Her pulse hiked. 'If you want to change the music you pr—'

'I want to raise the panels.'

She blinked. 'Raise them?' Spoil the atmosphere she'd created with so much care and anticipation? But she knew by his demeanour not to argue. 'Green button, top left.'

The panels rose. The rain had eased and watery afternoon sunshine filtered in, highlighting the stark features of the man standing in front of her. Black pricks of stubble on his tight jaw, steely resolution in his eyes, those usually full lips compressed into a line.

Had she thought she'd influenced his decision to come back? She was no longer so sure. He didn't look like a man being coerced into doing something he didn't want to do as he tossed the remote onto the mat alongside his jacket. He looked like a man in control. What was worse, he was calling the shots—and Breanna was doing his bidding.

She found herself almost wilting under his scrutiny and drew herself up. 'I—'

'Don't. Don't say anything.'

For emphasis, or because he no doubt expected a fulsome retort from her, he reached out, pressed a thumb against her lips. He wrapped the other hand around her hair, twisted it around his wrist, forcing her to look up at him. 'We're going to do this my way.' He slid his thumb slowly along the seam of her lips. 'No messing about in dark corners.' He jutted his chin toward the windows where the light poured in then looked back into her eyes so there was no escaping that gaze. 'I want to see you well and properly while we do it.'

And she didn't say anything because, possibly for the first time in her life, she was speechless. Dumbstruck with a trembling and new kind of anticipation that swirled through her body. Gobsmacked because this wasn't happening how she'd planned. This was not how it was supposed to happen.

He gave her no time, laying a firm mouth on hers with ruthless and practised precision, sending tingles from her lips to the soles of her bare feet.

Her hands, which had hung useless at her sides for the past couple of moments, rose to his belt buckle only to be brushed aside by a strong hand. He lifted his lips barely enough to remind her, 'My way.'

'B—'

Okay. She closed her eyes and allowed herself to be swept away by pure sensation. Her breasts felt full, swollen, her nipples tight, and she wished he would just soothe the ache—anyhow he liked. She breathed in the scent of warm man and sandalwood. The slow seductive sound of blue moon jazz cruised on the air.

Crushing her mouth, he hauled her closer. *Finally.* All the way…pressed against him, from neck to knee and every place in between. His body was hot and hard, lean and fit. She moaned as his erection pushed against her belly, her hips instinctively arching to meet him.

Anticipation was pale comparison to the real deal and her body quivered, her heart catapulted against her ribs. She'd wanted more than a kiss with Leo, had imagined how it would feel but hadn't imagined it would ever be this intense. This raw, primitive need for him that transcended anything she'd ever felt before.

Releasing her, he drew back, watching her. He was breathing heavily, his eyes molten, his lips glistening from their assault on hers. 'I want you. In the daylight. No adornments, no frills. Just you.'

'Ever see me wearing a *frill*?' She had an insane desire to laugh but she couldn't seem to raise her voice above a murmur.

Humour glinted in his eyes. 'Good point.' His voice, however, was rough velvet and confident when he promised, 'I'm going to make you come.'

A glorious fist of desire slammed against her middle. *Thank the Lord.*

The backs of his fingers trailed shivers down her bare arm. 'I'm going to watch you while you do.'

Damp heat spurted low in her belly and she felt her tangerine lace panties grow damp. 'Yes.'

'As you already know, I'm a man who likes to take his time, so we could be here a while.'

No problem at all. But she felt obliged to remind him. 'Your dinner appointment?'

He walked to the non-alcoholic bar in the corner, picked up a stool. 'I've rescheduled.' Setting it in front of her, he sat down, hands on his thighs, fingers splayed, his gaze sending sparks all down her body. 'Wet road, poor visibility. It's a supper meeting now.'

'Ah...'

He'd rescheduled for her—for both of them—as she'd expected he would. But this man caressing her up and down with hot eyes and taking his time... She felt almost gauche and inexperienced, which was amazing and odd since she was always an eager and equal participant in her sexual encounters.

This was new. She licked her lips, tasted him. Couldn't stand the tension a second longer. 'So, are we going to get on with it?'

His eyes sparked with heat as he gestured with a jerk of his chin. 'Get rid of the dress.'

'You don't want to do it yourself?'

He shifted his position, spreading his thighs a little. 'I'd prefer to watch.'

Satisfied with that response, she smiled, untied the halter neck and let it shimmer down her body.

Fascination held Leo immobile as he watched the garment slide down, down, down. It caught for an instant on her breasts, then with a little wiggle it shimmied, light and shadow playing on its silky surface as it revealed the curve of her slender waist. A flat belly, then, to his surprise, a miniature strawberry stud twinkled at her navel. Something to talk about some other time.

Then those endlessly long legs he hadn't been able to stop fantasising about. Damn shame he wouldn't have time for the steamy spa she'd obviously planned for the two of them.

Like all women, he supposed she'd worn the sexy underwear for his pleasure. And he appreciated it. But it could only mean she'd thought about having sex with him. Not only thought about it—she'd anticipated it. Unless she always dressed prepared for a little seduction?

Either that or she'd *known* he'd come back... Something he hadn't known himself until a short time ago. And in that time, she'd showered and changed—he'd smelled fresh soap on her skin and a spritz of her midnight temptation perfume. And her choice of dress was chosen expressly for slipping off. The knowledge disturbed him more than he was comfortable with.

Who was playing who?

He twirled a finger in the air. 'Turn around.' He had the upper hand, at least for now.

Arms outstretched, she pirouetted while he admired firm, round buttocks. His palms tingled—tempting little handfuls he was itching to familiarise himself with some more. Her lingerie choice came a distant second to all that pretty skin. 'Nice colour,' he told her. 'Hot.'

'Like a sunrise,' she said with the confident smile that had no doubt seduced countless would-be lovers.

Seduced. 'Come here,' he demanded, absurdly annoyed with her self-assurance and his thoughts of her with other men. Annoyed, because jealous was not a word he associated with himself. Ever.

As she glided closer he wondered how long he could go without touching her.

He discovered the answer two quick heartbeats later when he slid his hands around her waist. He was right: her skin felt like warm silk and his fingers wandered up her ribcage, thumbs flicking over the underside of her breasts through her bra. Tight, wine-dark nipples pressed against the lace, temptingly erect, tantalisingly close. His erection throbbed in time with his pulse and he was glad he was sitting down. He breathed deep and slow and dug down deep for that last remnant of control.

Her hands rose to cover his. 'Let's—'

'Hands behind your neck. Clasped.'

She made a whimpering sound but did as instructed, which pushed her breasts closer, an irresistible provocation.

Pulling her to him, he closed his mouth around one nipple and sucked her through the lace, drawing the tight bullet into his mouth while he manipulated and drew out the other between thumb and forefinger.

And in those few stuttering heartbeats, nothing but naked skin would suffice. He leaned back to look at her, more than satisfied with the view. Desire and desperation in her eyes, cheeks flushed with arousal, lips parted. Hands still clasped behind her head.

Satisfied? Leo choked back a laugh. Hell, he wasn't nearly satisfied. His head spun with her scent, her taste and every part of his body screamed for more. For all.

Not yet.

He reached out to touch again and his infamous control slipped a notch. More. *To hell with it.* One swift tug and her panties were gone, rent in two and tossed over his shoulder. He glimpsed the shock in her eyes but he was already grasping that final flimsy barrier in his fist.

Brie gasped as the last of her clothing was shredded and flung who knew where. Not in fear, not in fury or indignation, but with rising excitement. His gaze swept over her naked body, raising goosebumps upon goosebumps. Dizzy with desire, she swayed towards him, quivering, shivering, craving more.

He slammed both thighs with his fists. 'Come here.'

Yes. She didn't need to be told twice. Brie watched his eyes turn smoky as she straddled him, opened her most intimate self to his smouldering silver gaze, her limp arms all but collapsing onto his shoulders.

His hard masculine hand moved down between them. Biting down on her lower lip, she arched upwards, the ache, the tension in her lower belly almost unbearable. *Leo.* 'Touch me.' The words hissed out between clenched teeth.

He stroked her once, fingers gliding like silk over her moist centre, their gazes fused as he watched her gasp and shudder and moan at that first startling contact. Her attention drifted to where his fingers stroked, slow and steady, again and again. She could only whimper. The man rendered her incapable of speech, incapable of co-herent thought.

But she could feel that slow slide to paradise. Oh, *how* she could feel. Sensation building on glorious sensation. What Leo was doing to her went way beyond her wildest experience—and she'd had her share of wild experiences—yet paradoxically he was achieving it with his frustratingly leisurely patience. Barely touching her—as soothing and gentle as the misty rain on the other side of the windows.

She could smell the jasmine oil now, and magnificent man and her own arousal, could hear the fast thud of her heart, and, despite his keeping his movements slow, Leo's quickened breathing. Then she heard him say, 'Look at me.'

'I am,' she murmured, her gaze riveted by the impres-sive erection straining against his jeans. *Oh, my.* She couldn't wait to wrap her hands around him but her own needs took precedence when he pushed a finger inside. She bit her lip and pleaded, 'Hurry, hurry, hurry.'

He did *not* oblige. 'No. Right now I want slow and wet and slippery. And I want to watch your eyes when I take you there so *look at me.*'

His words thrilled, excited, electrified. She lifted her gaze. His brow was dotted with sweat, his grim-mouthed expression telling her how much effort it was costing him to hold onto that control he seemed determined to main-tain.

Mindless passion, a sweet lingering endurance. They

watched each other as he took her higher, pressure building, slowly at first, then gaining momentum. Faster, faster
on her own runaway sky rocket.

He sent her soaring to heaven before she could scream
hallelujah.

It took a couple of stuttering heartbeats to reclaim some
shred of sanity, her arms trembling, hands clutching his
shoulders, his mohair jumper soft against her fingers.
'You...' she barely managed. 'Inside.'

She heard the rasp of his zip, the rustle of foil as he
protected them both and still his eyes didn't leave hers. It
was as if some force had brought them together and refused to let go.

He drove himself home in one fierce thrust, the force
expelling what little breath was left in her body. She raised
her hands to shoulder height, palms facing forward, and
exhilarated in the power she felt in the fingers that linked
with hers. Murmured his name as they rocked together
towards that final glorious peak.

She felt his release deep inside, her internal muscles
rippling around him in response as she climaxed a second time. On a shuddering groan, he threw back his head,
exposing the strong masculine curve of jaw and stubbled
chin.

Spent, she collapsed over him with a satisfied moan.
Finally, a man with the determined will to rival hers in
the bedroom—or wherever else they chose to do it. Until
Leo had come into her life, she'd not realised this sexual
power-play with a worthy opponent was what she'd missed
in a lover.

Not just sex, a tiny voice whispered. Something deeper.

Wasn't going to happen.

She caught sight of her ruined bra floating in the spa
and clutched at the distraction like a woman drowning.
'No appreciation for sexy underwear?' she murmured.

'Not so much as for what lies beneath it.'

His answer was just what she needed, keeping her in the now. Sexy and casual—what they both wanted. She'd have grinned but her face felt numb. 'That was my newest pièce de résistance.'

He pushed up, bringing her to her feet so suddenly she almost stumbled. 'I'll pay for the damages.'

'Hey, I wasn't complaining.'

'Nevertheless. Bathroom?' He was tucking himself away; his tone bordered on curt.

'Door on the left.' Brie pointed towards the far side of the pool. Was it her overactive hormones or was it the feeling that everything had just changed, making him seem remote and in a hurry to leave?

Her nakedness in contrast to his fully dressed state added to her intense feeling of vulnerability.

Of course he'd be in a hurry, she told herself, grabbing her dress and hauling it up her bare torso. He had a three-hour drive in slippery conditions. He'd be driving through dusk then full dark with heavy cloud and possible fog. The country roads would be horrendous if the rain started up again, as it threatened to.

He exited the bathroom looking casual and gorgeous and her heart did an unexpected somersault in her chest. She'd got what she'd wanted but she'd not factored in the serious cardio workout that had come with it.

She didn't need cardio; she got that at the gym. Especially not with him. He was short-term, like her. They both understood that. 'Are you sure it's wise to travel tonight?'

'You'd advise against it?'

'Yes. You could—'

'You think like a girl.' He swiped his jacket up off the mat.

'I *think* like someone who's concerned about you.'

He looked genuinely surprised, eyes widening as they

flicked to hers, fingers motionless for an instant on the soft leather. 'Don't be. I've been looking after myself since I was five years old.' His lips quirked as he shrugged it on. 'I've scored a suite in Heaven for tonight and I don't intend to waste it.'

Focused on his six-star accommodation. Not a word about whether the earth had moved for him. No suggestion of when, or even if, they might do it again. After such an orgasmic interlude, for her at least, he made Brie feel more than a little idiotic.

And she *was* an idiot to make such a big deal of it. 'Well, enjoy,' she said, making herself smile and be her usual laid-back self. 'I know I would.'

'Hey, you're in a good spot—what's not to enjoy here?'

'Absolutely. And I will.' She'd make sure she did.

'I'll contact you.'

Ha. Of course he would. She relaxed into her smile. 'I'll be here. Not that it matters where I am. The beauty of mobiles.'

'Yeah.' Quick flash of humour in his eyes. 'Because I need your banking details for the rental payments.'

Oh. 'Right. Fine.'

A small frown pinched his brow. 'Problem?'

'Not at all,' she said, tightly. Angry. And doubly angry that she felt the absolute need to lie but in this instance her damaged pride and her rare attack of vulnerability demanded it.

'Good, then.' He flipped a hand. 'Stay warm, I'll see myself out.' He turned, walked towards the main wing. 'Catch you later.'

Not if she could help it. But even as she muttered, 'Right,' she knew that wasn't true. Thin-lipped, she hugged her bare arms and watched him disappear, listened to his footsteps fade. 'Damn you, Leo Hamilton. You made me lie.'

It didn't matter, she reminded herself. *He* didn't matter.

It was just sex—spectacular, mind-blowing, earth-shattering sex. But that was all it was. *Had been,* she told herself, because there'd be no repeat performance.

Remember, Brie: No heart, no hurt.

CHAPTER EIGHT

LEO HAD MORE important things to think about. He repeated it over and over. More important things than the woman who'd stripped his mind clean of everything except having her again any which way he could. He crossed the Derwent Bridge for the second time in as many hours, relieved he had somewhere he needed to be and he needed to be there fast. Clients to impress, a reputation to uphold.

Business was his focus. His priority. His life. *Never forget it.*

His tyres sprayed water and brakes screeched as he hit them for a red light he'd not seen till the last second. Leo shook his head and glared at the wet road in front of him. *See what happens when you allow yourself to be side-tracked by a woman?*

No, sir. Not Leo Hamilton, happy-go-lucky bachelor. He had enough trouble handling his sister. Safest to keep relationships with the opposite sex simple, easy, uncomplicated.

Not so easy. Because he couldn't stop himself wondering what the woman he'd left behind less than thirty minutes ago was doing now. Indulging in a soak in her steamy spa or a vintage champagne from her brother's rare and expensive French collection? Given her mood when he'd departed, it was more likely champagne *in* that steamy spa.

She'd be hard at work, soaking her sulk away in a mountain of froth, because every man knew when a woman said 'fine' in a tone that could slice through an iceberg at fifty paces, she meant anything but.

Precisely the reason he liked his single, uncomplicated life. Never get involved with a woman's sulks. He knew Breanna had expected the afternoon to continue into the evening. He'd been sorry to have to disappoint because he'd have enjoyed the promised sex in the spa as well as the next guy, but work took priority. There'd be other opportunities.

She'd not been able to get enough of him.

He smiled, remembering. But his smile faded. Was pleasure all it had been? Nowhere near an adequate description, but the alternative was too unsettling to contemplate.

She'd expected more from him. He'd been too afraid of his own reaction to stay. And why would he stay? He was late already.

Switching the radio station from jazz to pop, he shook the edgy feeling away and tapped along with the beat, overtaking a semi-trailer as he travelled through rolling farmland beneath a bruised evening sky and rehearsed the agenda for tonight's meeting aloud to keep his concentration focused where it should be.

But it wasn't long before his thoughts returned to Breanna and a pressing desire to hear her voice. 'Call Breanna Black on her mobile number,' he told his smartphone. Then changed his mind when he heard the ring tone. 'Cancel that call.' Because what would he tell her? That the sex had been incredible? That she was the most responsive lover he'd ever had? She had a body that could keep a man awake and tossing into the wee hours?

She'd be keeping him awake tonight.

And there it was again, plain as the purple clouds on the horizon. *He'd* not been able to get enough of *her*.

He swore once—loudly—then, still muttering, shook

his head. She'd made it clear she couldn't wait and he'd been so besotted with her uninhibited self-confidence, her sheer abandonment when she'd come apart in his arms, he'd not even considered his own reaction.

Or deliberately chosen not to.

He remembered that instant when he'd linked his fingers through hers as he pushed slowly inside her for the first time. A fleeting notion that he'd been waiting his whole life for that moment... He dragged a nervous hand over his head. All just another facet of her mysterious charm, he assured himself, but he had to work hard to shove it to the back of his mind. Tonight he had a job to do.

The following morning, Leo breakfasted on juice, sweetcorn fritters with smoked Tasmanian salmon and a giant kick-start espresso coffee in Heavenly View, one of Heaven's three restaurants. The table overlooked the ocean where the morning star hung like a jewel and a thin line of approaching daylight spread along a pearl horizon.

Experiencing the newest six-star eco-lodge first-hand had well and truly lived up to his expectations. The only structure approved within thirty-five kilometres, it perched on a hill forty metres above a pounding sea and pristine white beaches. The team had done a great job blending conservation and tourism while protecting the coastal wilderness. The building materials had been choppered in, the sumptuous dining experience used fresh local produce exclusively.

He'd established new benchmarks for sustainable tourism including conversion of waste into clean irrigation water and an extensive recycling programme. He'd also kick-started the establishment of a fund supporting local environmental projects, the final details of which he'd laid out to the team last night.

This morning he was basking in the afterglow of success and a hefty five-figure deposit was due in his bank balance. Further, in appreciation of his work, he'd received a complimentary weekend break for two starting Friday evening with a seven-course gastronomic delight to be served in the most expensive suite the lodge had to offer.

He glanced at his phone, screen black against the snowy white tablecloth. His first thought on waking had been of Breanna and whether she'd slept as little as he. In the next moment, he'd wanted to share his good news and tell her his efforts over the past ten months had been rewarded and to ask if she was free this coming weekend.

Which was totally unexpected because he'd never felt the desire to share any aspect of his business or its success with any woman. Never mixed business with pleasure.

But the weekend of indulgence on offer was a different matter, he told himself as he flicked through the day's news on his tablet. It had to be this coming weekend because he'd arranged to be in Singapore on business for the next, and three weeks was ridiculously too far away. However, phoning a woman at six a.m. smacked of desperation. One thing Leo had never been was desperate.

A text, then, asking her if she was free, which she could read at her leisure. He shook his head. He'd call in and see her on his way home. She'd be at work…

He drummed his fingers on the tablecloth and glared at his phone again. What was happening to him? Until yesterday afternoon he'd considered himself a reasonably sophisticated guy when it came to women and the whole dating scene. Well, the jury was out on that one now.

Nor had he ever been gripped by indecision. *Just do it.* He reached for the phone at the same time it rang in his hand. Sunny's photo beamed back at him.

He beat back the tiny disappointment that it wasn't Breanna. And instantly castigated himself. 'Hey, Suns.' Hearing her voice raised a momentary concern. Sunny rarely rang him—it was always the other way round. 'Everything okay?'

'Everything's great. Only four days to go to the big Opera House gig. I'm super excited now.'

'I bet.' He relaxed as the tension eased with Sunny's bright enthusiasm. 'So what are you up to so early this morning?'

'Extra violin practice, but I should be asking you that question.'

He straightened in his dining chair as the tension crept back. 'What did I miss?'

'First up, you departed Melbourne a day earlier than you planned, with only a text to say you'd left. Then I don't hear from you for over forty-eight hours—you never let it go more than a day. What's going on?'

He picked up a butter knife, twirled it between his fingers and said, 'You expressed a need for space, said I was stifling you. "Control freak" has been tossed out there a few times, amongst other things.'

'Yeah, all well and good but since when have you listened to me, brother love? So who's the woman?'

'If you believe there's a woman involved, why are you checking up on me at the crack of dawn? It's still dark, for Pete's sake.'

'Shall I ring back later, then?' she asked, sweetly.

'No. I'm not with a woman. I'm in Heaven.'

'In heaven without a woman? That's not like you, Leo.'

'Sunny dearest.'

'Leo love. Who's the woman?' He opened his mouth but she spoke first. 'Never mind denying it. So—' her tone turned brisk '—how *is* Heaven?'

'Still looking pretty black from where I'm sitting.'

'Everything going okay over there?'

'Better than okay. I left home a day early because I needed to go over some minor adjustments in the kitchen

with my architect and I had some details to finalise before
the meeting here, which, by the way, was a major success.'

'Of course it was. Congratulations! Your architect's a
woman, right?'

'And your point is?'

'Never mind. Have you met any of my neighbours yet?'
Breanna.

His body responded with all too easily remembered
heat. Her face looking more stunned than stunning the last
time he saw her. In a shimmery dress that was all but trans-
parent from a certain angle; but of course she'd known that.

And the way she'd looked—the way he always left a
woman—dishevelled and satisfied.

Except, this time… Something inside him twisted. He
felt as if he'd left a tiny part of himself behind.

Since Sunny had specifically asked, there was no point
putting it off; he felt obliged to fill her in. 'I've met West
Wind's owner.' He cleared a husk from his throat. 'As it's
turned out, I'll be staying there for a bit when I'm down in
Hobart while she house-sits for her brother and his wife.
So I'm right next door to our place. Convenient all round.'

'Yes. Very convenient.'

'She's absolutely not my kind of woman,' he stated.
Too fast, too curtly.

'Did I ask?'

At the humour in her voice, he swore beneath his breath
while leaping to his own defence. 'She's extroverted and
argumentative.' *And sexy and honest and too intriguing
for his own peace of mind.* 'The kind of woman who'd
drive any sane man crazy. You two should get on well.'

'Really? Interesting. Are you a sane man, brother love?'

'You tell me,' he said, tapping the knife repeatedly on
the tablecloth. He'd thought he was. Now he wasn't so sure.
Brie had done that to him. They'd spent a handful of hours
together over the past couple of weeks and Breanna had

changed who he was in some way. She'd worked her unique and magic brand of seduction. How had he let that happen?

'You're so sane it's scary,' Sunny said. 'So, does *she* have a name?'

'Breanna Black. Beauty therapist with her own business. Eve's Naturally. Into natural stuff.' *Tisanes*—whatever the hell they were. Foody face masks. 'Talks to her plants.' His mind wandered back to that first weekend. 'They call her Party Babe Brie. Apparently. What does that tell you?'

'That she's fun?'

'Exactly my point,' he muttered. 'I don't have time to waste.' Not that he didn't enjoy fun—he did—but being with Breanna was like being on a wild ride at an amusement park and he'd never enjoyed that out-of-control, falling sensation at the top of a roller coaster...

'You've been avoiding her, then.'

'Yes. No. Not exactly. Listen, I have to get moving,' he told her, tossing down the knife and pushing back his chair, *needing* to end this conversation *now*. 'Some loose ends to tie up here before I leave.'

'Okay. Friday night, don't be late. I have too much to do to worry about reminding you.'

'In which case, I'll not intrude on your precious time for the rest of the week,' he said, making his way out of the restaurant.

She laughed. 'I'll be the girl in the sparkly black dress.'

'Ciao, for now.' He disconnected, almost walked into Heaven's senior accountant at the door. 'Gerald, good morning. I was hoping to see you before I leave,' he said, relieved to switch to business. 'I need another look at those figures.'

Because he was always straight with Sunny—except when it came to her sexy new neighbour—he made sure to find a few more of those loose ends before leaving Heaven.

They took longer than he'd anticipated and he made a couple of overseas calls to other clients so he had no time to phone that sexy neighbour until nine-thirty when he was halfway back to Hobart.

He called up her number, heard it ring, tapped his fingers impatiently. 'Come on, Breanna, pick up.'

'Hello. You've reached Breanna Black. I'm unable to take your call...' He let the sound of her low, sensual voice wash over him and tried to curb his impatience. He wanted to hear that voice up close and in person and moaning sexy things, not a detached greeting on some mechanical device. 'Please leave your name and a message and I'll return your call as soon as possible.'

'Leo speaking. Don't bother returning my call. I'll be at your salon in about ninety minutes.'

Brie took a mid-morning break in the lunch room she shared with Sam and Lynda, a physiotherapist. She wished she were fully booked and too busy for distractions today but her next client had cancelled. So she intended catching up on client info in preparation for the upcoming move to the retreat. She blew on her blackberry tea as she scrolled through her messages one-handed and saw she'd missed a call from the biggest distraction of all.

Her heart did a back-flip against her ribs, her palms instantly sweaty, and she almost dropped the phone. Her finger was poised to retrieve the voice message when she remembered. Leo—her new *tenant*—had said he'd contact her about banking details for the rent. As he'd all but bolted out of the door.

She plunked her mobile on the table, glared at it and took a sip of too-hot tea while she waited impatiently for her heart to settle down. She didn't want to hear his message. Why put herself through the humiliation and sheer awkwardness of hearing him ask about *banking details*?

She'd text him the information instead—now—so he wouldn't have to call back.

What was wrong with her that he'd obviously decided sex between them wasn't going to work? Yes, he'd been in a hurry for an appointment he'd postponed—for her. No. She crossed her arms, still glaring at the phone. For them. But mostly for himself.

After she'd tempted him to play her game, it was true. But his lack of response after their close encounter had left her feeling inadequate and dissatisfied. A word, a touch, a kiss… Anything to let her know he'd felt *something*.

She'd never had sex with a man who hadn't wanted more. And knowing that, she'd always held the power; she'd set the rules. Her rules. No-strings sex for as long as it worked for both of them and exclusivity while they were doing it.

Her rules didn't seem to work with Leo, who obviously set his own. She'd known that and had gone ahead and played anyway. With a man she realised now she didn't understand as well as she'd thought.

It was time to stop thinking, time to get moving. Brie drained her cup then rinsed it in the little sink. A quick draught alerted her to a presence behind her. Turning, she saw Leo just inside the room.

'The receptionist? Jodie?' He jerked a thumb over his shoulder. 'She said I could come on back.'

Brie just bet she did. It was a wonder she hadn't shown him the way personally.

'She offered to show me the way but I didn't want to waste time on polite conversation or wait while the both of you engage in useless office talk.'

'Okay.' She ripped off a piece of paper towel and wiped her mug with exaggerated care and was pleased to note the tightness in his jaw, the way he stood, fingers tense against his thighs. Fingers that had stroked her all the way to heaven mere hours before. 'What *do* you want to waste time on?'

'I wanted to see you alone. And I promise it won't be a waste of time.'

'No?'

'No.'

A tingle raced down her spine but, no matter how tempting his promise, she refused to play. Leo Hamilton needed to learn he couldn't treat women—her in particular—with such a cavalier attitude. 'So it's your lucky day,' she said with a smile, then tossed up her hands. 'Oops, too late. Break time's over.'

His lips compressed in obvious irritation. Without taking his eyes off her, he shut the door. 'Not yet. I juggled appointments to be here so—'

'Yeah, *so*? This is my place of work.'

'I know, I saw your office on the way through.' The way he spoke, she knew he wasn't impressed with the way she organised her desk—or not, as the case happened to be.

'*And* this room's a shared space,' she went on. 'I take my business reputation seriously and I have appointments too. You can't just—'

'Jodie told me your next client cancelled. You're free. So am I.'

'Am I supposed to be impressed that you've juggled your work to visit me here? Because it happens to suit you?'

'It doesn't suit, particularly, but I'm here anyway. To see you, as I've just explained.'

'Have you heard the saying, never mix business with pleasure?'

'Who said anything about business?' In two strides he was in front of her.

His fingers were firm and impatient on her shoulders

and excitement zipped down her spine, but she shrugged out of his grip. 'Who said anything about pleasure?'

'Breanna.' He spoke her name in a voice that was pure seduction with a glimmer of self-deprecating humour. 'You're annoyed with me.'

Yeah. Big time. 'How very perceptive of you.' To siphon her mad into positive energy she ripped off another square of paper towel, turned her back on him and began rubbing at tea stains on the sink.

'I had to leave, you knew that.'

'Yes.' She stopped, turned back and looked him straight in the eye. 'But it's the manner in which you left.' And the state he'd left her in.

He looked perplexed, brow furrowed. 'This is just sex with us, right? That's all you want? All either of us want,' he finished with a certain grim finality.

'Absolutely. Couldn't agree more.'

'So what's the problem?'

'A little post-coital conversation would have been…I think "polite" is the word I'm looking for. Maybe you're not familiar with the etiquette a woman expects after sex. Still, you could have stayed a few moments and proved me wrong.'

'Not when I have an important meeting I'm already running late for because I stayed longer than I should have with you. Longer than I meant to.'

'Okay.' Tossing the paper towel in the kitchen tidy, she swiped her tense fingers down the front of her navy skirt. 'So are you saying if you hadn't had that meeting scheduled, you'd have been happy to stick around? Be honest, please, because I got the distinct impression you couldn't wait to get out of there and I'd rather know now than be made a fool of.'

He nodded slowly, as if considering his words with care. 'I didn't sleep a wink in Heaven's softer-than-air bed last night; what do you think? And if you're under the impression I'd ever set out to deliberately make a fool of you, you couldn't be more wrong.'

He did appear a little worse for wear today, she noticed. Eyes bleary, lines etched deeper around his mouth. She sensed there was more he wasn't saying but she accepted his roundabout excuse for an apology for now, until she could get to the bottom of whatever it was that had disturbed him. Because he'd very neatly avoided her first question. 'I didn't sleep much either,' she confessed.

His smile was slow and shattering. 'I have something in mind I think you'll enjoy.'

To her shocked embarrassment she felt her cheeks *blooming* at his blatant promise of erotic delights. Like a teenager, for heaven's sakes. To hide it, she busied herself rinsing everyone else's coffee-stained mugs. 'I'm listening.'

'Is next weekend free for you?' he said close to her ear.

She pressed her lips together at the exciting sensation of her body vibrating in harmony with his voice. Struggled to answer with her usual flirty tone. 'It could be. If you make it worthwhile.'

'How about I take you to Heaven?'

A corner of her mouth lifted. 'You already have.'

'This'll be better. Sex *and* post-coital conversation with food and wine and stunning views. A weekend of heaven at Heaven. We can take our time returning after Sunday brunch. What do you say?'

Irresistible. How could she refuse? 'I say that sounds like a tempting offer, Mr Hamilton.'

'Make no mistake, Ms Black, it's a very tempting offer. Question is, are you going to take me up on it?'

'I reckon I might…'

'G—'

'Think about it,' she finished, with a smile on the inside.

Let him think about *that*. She stepped sideways to reach for the teapot but she found herself being spun around and pressed up against the kitchen bench by a hard, toned body.

Before she could utter another word, his lips crushed hers. His unique flavour was overlaid with impatience and desire, as if he couldn't get enough quickly enough and was damned annoyed about it.

To heck with fighting it, she decided, absorbing his hot, dark taste as his hands moved down her back, cupping her buttocks and dragging her closer to that hard ridge of masculine heat.

'What happened to slow?' she managed when he finally lifted his mouth to stare down at her.

'A change is good.'

Then somehow her skirt was ruched halfway up her thighs and her hands sliding like limp spaghetti over his shoulders. His hands were nowhere near as innocent, caressing her breasts outside her virginal white blouse, then rolling the hard nipples between his fingers as he tugged at an ear lobe with his teeth. 'Good?'

'Good.' Whimpering, she arched her back, rubbing her aching breasts against his palms, his rock-hard erection pressing against her belly. 'This is so *bad*...'

'Positively wicked.' His hands slid down her body, over her thighs, stroking her skin, then inching higher beneath the hem.

She smiled against his stubbled cheek. 'I like a bit of wicked.'

'I know.' He pulled away, staring at her with eyes that, for one fleeting instant, reminded her of a wolf with one foot caught in a trap. 'You're a fascinating enigma, Breanna Black.'

'And that bothers you.'

'I can handle it,' he muttered. 'And you.'

'I look forward to being handled,' she said. 'As long

as you're only referring to the bedroom. You're one very sexy man, Leo Hamilton, and, to my complete surprise, I find I like you. Shall we leave it at that?'

He fingered a strand of wayward hair at her temple that had escaped the clasp at the back of her head. 'I'll pick you up on Friday night. What time do you finish?'

'I'll be ready to leave by five. No, make it four-thirty. No sense waiting around—I'm an impatient woman.'

'So am I.' He slid a finger across her lips. 'Impatient, I mean.'

She sucked in a slow breath between her teeth. 'So, is this a dirty weekend or a romantic getaway?'

'What do you think?' He started to walk towards the door.

'I need to know what clothes to pack.'

He turned back. His gaze was molten silver, stroking over her. 'An overnight bag is all you'll need. And your contraceptive pill if you take it.'

Her pulse pounded, a carnival ride out of control. 'I do.'

'Glad to hear it.'

'Me too.' It was going to be okay. Just sex. Fun times. Temporary.

'I promise you a night you won't forget. Two, in fact.'

He grinned with wicked intent, which had her insides jumping erratically, and waved a hand towards her chest. 'But you might want to fix your blouse for now.'

Oh, cripes.

By the time she looked up again, he was gone.

CHAPTER NINE

Leo was flat out seeing clients in the north of the island state for the rest of the week. He had to adjust his schedule around losing Friday afternoon in order to drive back to Hobart then on to Heaven. There was no possibility of making up that time over the weekend because he intended spending every waking moment indulging in more fascinating pursuits.

Since he was working in a remote wilderness area west of Launceston, he had no mobile coverage from Wednesday morning onwards. Which was a good thing because it prevented him from picking up the phone late in the evening just to hear Brie's sensual bedroom voice and indulge in a little pillow talk to get him in the right mood for the weekend.

Not that he hadn't been in the right mood since he'd seen her on Monday morning at her office. He'd wanted her so badly his body ached. Still did. He'd not been able to focus properly on anything else since.

She was still a distraction he couldn't afford.

He reminded himself of that fact as he checked his phone messages at two p.m. on Friday. Moments ago he'd arrived back in Launceston and was taking a coffee break on the town's outskirts before driving on to Hobart.

Then he saw something that dashed his cheery anticipation into the ground. A check-in reminder for this afternoon's four-thirty p.m. flight to Sydney. Sent yesterday when he'd been out of range.

No freaking way.

His mood plummeted and he stared at the screen, disbelief tracking like tiny ice picks up his spine. *Not possible.* Sunny's concert was *next* Friday. It had to be—he'd booked the flight for the wrong week, that was all. But even as he brought his calendar up on the screen he remembered that next weekend he was due in Singapore.

He heard Sunny's voice echo in his ear from Monday morning's conversation. *Don't be late.*

And there it was—the ugly truth. Stabbing him in the eyes. Pounding away in his head. He was due in Sydney *this evening* to watch his baby sister perform at the Opera House. Sunny's dream gig—and now his waking nightmare.

He'd been so caught up with his own carnal needs and wants, he'd forgotten the person who deserved his support the most. Someone who deserved so much better than a brother who forgot her important day.

He slapped cash on the table and dashed to his car. Shoving it into gear, he all but fish-tailed out of the tiny café's driveway and headed south to Hobart. The airport was this side of town; he'd have to put his car in long-term parking overnight. If he drove straight there instead of going home to shower and change, he might just make it before the final passenger call.

Wasn't it ironic? His flight was departing Hobart at the same time he was due to pick up Breanna for their idyllic weekend away.

Brie squeezed her Friday afternoon clients in between the morning ones, forfeiting her morning tea and lunch break to do so.

She'd dashed out at three-thirty, and as she drove home

to change and get ready she hoped all the juggling was worth it.

It would be worth it.

As she hurried inside, she checked her mobile for the first time since midday and saw three missed calls from Leo, made every half-hour since two this afternoon. He'd not left a message so she had no idea what to make of them, but a bad feeling snaked through her gut. She was about to call him back when the phone rang. Leo's number.

'Hi.' Her voice sounded too breathless—she was aiming for casual. 'What's up?'

'Breanna.' She heard a pause, as if he wasn't sure how to say whatever it was. 'I apologise for the late notice but I can't make it this evening. I'm expected at an important function in Sydney and missing it is *not* an option.'

And here Brie was, thinking that their date was the most important event on his weekend's calendar. *Big mistake, Brie.* He didn't sound apologetic; he sounded terse, as if he couldn't wait to get off the phone. As if he made a habit of double booking and she rated a poor second after his work appointments. If indeed that was what it was… *Remember Elliot?* His appointments hadn't been work-related either.

Of course Brie wasn't an exception to a man like Leo. They weren't even in a proper relationship.

'It's only for tonight,' he went on when she didn't respond. 'I'll be back in Hobart tomorrow morning. It depends on flights, I need to change my booking. Thing is, my sis—'

'I was going to wash my hair anyway,' she cut in before she could hear his excuse. Her throat felt as if it was closing over—that old feeling she'd never wanted to suffer through again. 'No, I wasn't,' she said. 'I was going away with you, Leo Hamilton, because *you* invited *me*. But something better came up and you changed your mind.'

'I did *not* change my mind, Breanna. I messed up my diary and now they're calling my flight. Listen to me. My s—'

She disconnected, turned her phone off. For a moment she just stood and stared at the black screen as a chill wrapped around her. 'I don't want to hear your excuses,' she whispered through clenched teeth. 'I don't *want* to hurt the way Elliot made me hurt with his lies. The way my parents made me hurt with their secrets. And I know you could hurt me so much more than anyone else ever could.'

With the exception of her indulgent spa and champagne chill-out sessions, Brie didn't enjoy being on her own. If she had an evening free and found herself alone, she'd fill it: parties, work, colleagues, friends, distractions—it didn't matter.

That was the beauty of freedom. Freedom to choose what she did and who she did it with. Not being tied to a regular partner or schedule. Not having to be accountable to anyone but herself.

The only way to live. Right?

But tonight as darkness closed in, she couldn't focus on freedom or anything else. Leo had cancelled when she'd been looking forward to a weekend of fun and naughty surprises.

She needed something to take her mind off it.

Food, she decided, eyeing the fridge. The more calories and unhealthier, the better. She dug out two huge scoops of mango ripple ice cream, unwrapped the chocolate-coated almonds left over from last weekend's party and poked them in, then drizzled the lot with raspberry syrup.

She tucked in to the cold delight but Leo was still in her head. Something about the man tugged at her heart, and it terrified her. She wanted to believe he was a decent guy, an honest one. Like his concern for her safety when he'd had the fire alarm installed. For the umpteenth time tonight she wondered if she should have given him a chance to explain before he hopped on that plane to Sydney. To home.

Maybe the reason he lived with his sister was because she couldn't afford to live elsewhere, was jobless and had begged him to take her in? Brie never got involved in family issues with any guys she dated.

When the florist delivery service turned up on her security monitor with roses—four dozen yellow and a single black one with no card attached—her heart didn't stall or stop or turn cartwheels. It cramped. She redirected the driver to the local hospice. Grand gestures like that had always left her cold. It was too easy to order expensive flowers and forget the reason within moments. In her experience, flowers equalled a guilty conscience.

It was just the kind of thing her parents used to do. They'd toss a wad of cash at her and tell her to go spend it in the shopping mall, when all she wanted was for them to look her way. Nor had money bought friendships as a way out of her loneliness. She'd had to work hard for those.

Already overly full on ice cream, Brie poured herself a large glass of merlot. Setting it on the coffee table in front of the white leather lounge overlooking a forest of indoor plants, she put on a classical CD and found her knitting bag. She pulled out her home-spun alpaca yarn and in between mouthfuls of the ruby liquid she continued with what she called her stress scarf.

Leo's roses and the hospice threw up memories she'd never be able to forget. In his final hours at that hospice her father had revealed she had a half-brother.

The truth had changed her life. Clarified so much. Her whole life she'd been invisible to her parents and when her mother had been killed in a car accident nine years ago, Brie realised she'd never really known her.

Why couldn't they have just been honest?

All those missing years not knowing Jett hurt the most

of all. She knitted faster, needles clacking rhythmically like a train gathering speed.

Her parents' marriage had taught her what not to do so she'd made sure to end a relationship before she reached anything that might lead to deepening feelings. Until she'd met Elliot and made an exception—and what a disaster that had turned out to be. Which was why she'd be telling Leo it was over—because she was teetering on that dangerous edge again.

Falling for him wasn't an option. She loved her freedom, her lifestyle. She'd die of boredom if she was to commit herself to one man. Or so she told herself.

Totally out of sorts, she picked up her phone, tapped Samantha's number. When Sam answered, Brie didn't bother with preliminaries. 'What are you doing tonight?' then, 'Can I sleep over at your place? And you'll need to pick me up because I'm already over the limit.'

'You really care about this guy,' Sam said, over her margarita cocktail an hour later.

They'd found an out-of-the-way table in a chic bar with a view over Sullivans Cove—sheer luck for a normally busy ten o'clock on a Friday night.

'No. Yes. I don't want to. You know me—terminal party girl, no emotional entanglements. I'm not going to see him again.'

'Bit hard since you're his landlady and he's your next-door neighbour.'

'He's going to rent out his place when it's finished. All I'll see of him are his nice regular deposits into my bank account for the next few weeks or months, which will go to Pink Snowflake. So yay.'

Leaning on her elbows, Brie sucked a weak gin and tonic through her straw and stared at the waterfront and its light-rippling reflections. 'He cancelled our hot week-end—which I never asked for in the first place, by the way—for some unmissable function in Sydney.'

'Did he explain what it was?'

'I hung up on him before he could.'

'Brie. You have to stop doing that.'

'I can't deal with excuses and lies and rejection.'

'So you hung up and now you don't know if it was any of those or not.'

Brie slid a finger over the moisture on her glass. 'He's not into parties. See? He's just not my type.'

'Actually, I don't. He ticks all your boxes: looks, intelligence, charisma. So what if he doesn't like parties?'

'He prefers parties for two,' she murmured, then glanced sideways at Sam who was watching her with a smirk.

'There you are—he *is* your type.'

Brie looked back at the view. 'He sent roses.'

Sam slapped a hand on the table. 'The nerve of the man.'

'Flowers imply guilt.'

'Or an apology.'

'Or an easy out—call a florist, place an order and two minutes later the conscience is eased and the lucky recipient's forgotten.' Brie twisted in her chair to implore, 'Can we do lunch tomorrow? Just you and me. We can go to Salamanca first, I know you love the markets.'

'I've never seen you go to so much trouble *not* to see a guy who's obviously as interested in you as you are in him. And to be perfectly frank, I don't think you're being fair. At least give the guy a chance to explain.'

Brie shook her head. But Sam was right. Probably. 'I'm afraid of what I'll do if I do.'

Sam reached over and squeezed her hand. 'Okay. We'll do brunch and the markets, but the moment he contacts you and turns up—because you *will* tell him where we are, and he *will* turn up—you two are on your own.'

* * *

Sydney's fog was still hanging around but the curtain
was beginning to lighten, the runway almost visible now.
In the airport lounge, Leo shuffled his newspaper and
checked the departure board. His flight was still delayed
by at least an hour. He sent another text advising Breanna
since her phone was still switched off. He was learning
that it was Breanna's modus operandi. She was going to
have to change because he didn't like it. Further, he wasn't
going to put up with it.

She'd not given him a chance to explain and that was
unacceptable. What the hell did she want from him? He'd
had a floral arrangement delivered; he'd never known a
woman who couldn't be persuaded with flowers. And very
expensive they'd been too. But she'd remained stubbornly
out of contact.

Breanna was untidy, confrontational and too out there
for his taste. She was hard work. Why couldn't he forget
her and move on since that was what she seemed to want?
What made her so special that he couldn't wait to see her
again? Or maybe that was what it was—those differences,
those points of disagreement that challenged him.

And just to complicate things the other woman in his
life was also intruding on his thoughts.

Before he'd left for the airport this morning, Leo had
stopped by Darling Harbour at Sunny's invitation to have
breakfast with her and the rest of Tasmania's Hope Strings
ensemble who were also in Sydney to see last night's Opera
House performance.

He'd been glad because he'd wanted an opportunity to
meet the people his sister would be working with. Ensure
she was accepted and happy. And from everything he'd
observed, she looked radiant with a glow to her cheeks
he'd never seen. She'd found her niche, so it was all good.
Fantastic.

But he'd noticed one guy paying particular attention to her. Gregor Goldsworthy had spiked hair with a greenish hue about it, a piercing in his left eyebrow, a tattoo on the inside of his wrist—and who knew where else since the rest of his upper body was covered in some sort of long sheepskin coat that looked as if it had been resurrected from the sixties.

He was fine with that. Live and let live. The respected cello player obviously scrubbed up okay when a formal occasion demanded it. And Sunny was an attractive, out-going and talented blonde; of course men were going to notice her.

But what Leo couldn't get past was the fact that Sunny had been paying this Gregor guy the same rapt attention. The knowledge stirred uncomfortably inside him like the curdled airport coffee he'd just disposed of.

Sunny hadn't mentioned Gregor—and why would she? She'd tell Leo to butt out of her private life. And he did. Mostly. Ditching his newspaper, he stalked to the windows where the sun was struggling through the rapidly dissi-pating fog. Ground crews were starting to move, the dis-embodied airport voice was announcing the first flights.

Time to go and have it out with Breanna.

Sam grabbed Brie's phone off the table where they were having brunch, checked it with a cluck of her tongue. 'You can only receive when it's switched *on*.'

'I've been checking,' Brie told her around a morsel of toast, since she was barely hungry. 'He texted his flight's due in at one-thirty. Fog delay. I switched it off so I don't have to talk to him.'

'Why'd you do that?' she asked, still playing with Brie's phone. She snapped a selfie of the two of them. 'You're the most confident woman I know when it comes to talk-ing with men.'

'Not this time.'

She gulped her English breakfast tea. Why was it different with him? Brie had never felt so spun out after having one-off sex. Since those amazing moments with Leo she felt as if she'd been ripped open and all her insecurities laid bare. Had anything changed between them in the meantime? If so, how would she deal with it?

She didn't know yet because she hadn't let him explain.

Of course, if he had changed his mind she'd deal with it. If he'd lied and she found out, she'd tell him where to go. But deep down, whatever the reason, she'd die a little. A lot.

Because no matter how hard she tried to deny it, it *mattered* with him. Nerves were so bunched up in her throat that she could barely talk. 'I need some air,' she muttered. 'This place is stifling.'

'Let's stroll down to the markets,' Sam said, handing her back her phone. 'He'll ring when he arrives and you can tell him to meet us there. That way it won't look like you've been sitting around waiting for him to show up.'

'Which I haven't been.' Brie made a determined effort to improve her mood for Sam's sake. 'I'm just enjoying a lazy morning out with a girlfriend.'

The day was chilly and grey but Saturday's regular tree-lined Salamanca Market in Hobart was a sensory hive of activity. The aromas of pancakes and burgers filled the air. Umbrellas sheltering stalls displaying everything from carpets and cloth to bird feeders and lampshades set against the backdrop of historic Georgian warehouses.

When her phone jingled in her pocket just after two o'clock, Brie startled. She yanked it out, checked caller ID, and her pulse went into overdrive. 'Leo.'

'How do you like your crêpes?' His voice was caramel-smooth. 'Lemon and sugar or strawberry jam?'

She spun around, saw him at the food tent a few stalls

away. He had his back to her but he stood out; an unmiss-able head above the rest. To add to her agitation, her whole body readied itself at the sight, as if it were programmed to respond exclusively to him. 'How did you know I'd be here?' She looked at Sam as she spoke.

'Forgotten your text already?'

'Traitor,' she whispered to Sam and turned away to watch a busker playing French songs on his piano accordion.

'What was that?' Leo's voice.

'I was speaking to Samantha. *She* was the one who texted you. I'll have the jam, please. And stay where you are. I'll come to you.' She disconnected with a scowl. 'Bet all the women say that to him. As for *you,* my friend, I'll haul you over the coals later.' But she let Sam give her a quick hug before she made her way through the crowd.

She thought she was ready—calm and composed—when she tapped him on the shoulder and he turned around, his hands filled with crêpes, shiny dark hair riffling in the breeze.

And then she was leaning over to kiss his cheek, inhaling his warm scent before she could think about it.

Before she remembered yesterday.

'Hi.' She pulled back, stared into pewter eyes that reflected the sombre morning sky. 'I shouldn't have hung up on you last night.'

'I've noticed you do that a lot.'

She heard the disappointment in his tone. 'Yes. I know, and I'm sorry.'

'Is it a bad habit of yours or is it just me?'

'It's not you.' She clenched her hands, rubbed them together, not from cold but with nerves. 'Are you going to accept my apology or not?'

'I will. This time.'

His gaze grew so intense she had to force herself not to

flinch and look away. 'I know I didn't listen yesterday but I do want to know why you cancelled on me.'

His expression remained inscrutable, as if he was deciding whether to tell her or not. Finally he nodded. 'Okay.' He looked about them. 'Let's find somewhere quieter.'

'That way.' She gestured away from the crowds to the top of Salamanca Place where there were seats beneath a canopy of trees.

'I got the roses,' she said, to fill the silence between them as they walked. 'Pretty.'

'Glad you think so.'

'Expensive.'

'Not a worry.'

'What was the black one symbolic of?'

'Me? Your light to my shadow? Wh—'

'I sent them to a hospice.'

His steps slowed a little. 'You sent them to a hospice.'

'I know some of the patients there and know they'd appreciate them far more than me.'

'Okay. You don't like flowers—got it.' He didn't say more as he led her to a seat on a grassy spot beneath some trees, handed her the plate with the jam-laced crêpe, kept the lemon and sugar one for himself.

'I love flowers. Just not for apologies.' Her stomach was churning but she unpeeled the plastic wrap and picked off a corner of her pancake. 'So?' she prompted.

'As I tried to explain before you cut me off, I messed up my diary. Rather, I didn't add you to my diary because, frankly, I didn't need to. I couldn't think of anything—or any*one*—else. Which got me into all sorts of—'

'You promised me a night I wouldn't forget. You were right—I won't forget.'

'Breanna…'

She held up her hand, looked away to the sandstone buildings around Sullivans Cove so she wouldn't read what she might in his gaze. 'I've changed my mind. I don't want to know.' She didn't want to hear. Was too scared to hear. 'I'm sure you had a perfectly valid reason, but this thing between us, it's not going to work, best not to go any further.' She rewrapped her virtually untouched crêpe in plastic and struggled against nausea. And fear. Oh, God, the fear. 'I'm not going to Heaven with you, Leo.'

His sudden iron-like grip on her upper arm through her thick jacket had her jolting and swivelling her head his way. Her paper plate slipped off her lap and onto the grass.

'Listen to me, Breanna.' His eyes were stormy, his mouth a grim slash, the powerful image of this man on the edge of his steely control setting Brie's heart pounding with something between exhilaration and anger.

'Take your hand off me,' she warned through clenched teeth.

But instead of letting her go, his fingers tightened. 'Listen to me first. Weeks ago I made a commitment to watch my little sister perform at the Opera House. Can you put yourself in my place a moment and imagine how I felt when I realised I'd been so preoccupied, so infatuated, so obsessed with *you,* Breanna Black, that I'd forgotten I was supposed to turn up and show my support on one of the biggest nights of her life? Leo Hamilton, the only family Sunny has—the only family I have.'

Brie exhaled slowly, searching his eyes, falling into that confused gaze. Falling for him a little more with every passing second that he punished himself as he loosened his grip on her arm, then let her go altogether with a muttering of disgust obviously aimed at himself.

'You went to watch your sister. And you nearly forgot because you were thinking about me.' The wonder of it stole through her heart like gold. 'I should've let you explain.'

'Yes.'

'You didn't forget in the end and that's all that matters,' she said, watching the tension in his shoulders ease
a little. 'You were there for her. What was Sunny doing at
the Opera House?'

'She's a violinist.'

'Talented. You must be a proud brother.'

'Yes. And you hung up on me because...?'

'Because I didn't want to hear your lies. What I expected would be lies.'

'Your opinion of me is that low?' He shook his head.

'No. I...'

'You have trust issues. What did he do?'

She nodded, glad he'd guessed because it made it easier
to tell him. 'A few years ago I was involved with a guy.
Foolishly blinded by his dazzling attention. Until I learned
that Elliot sent flowers whenever he cancelled his dates
with me to fool around with other women.'

'Despite the popular rumour, not all men are bastards,
Breanna.' He scowled, his expression dark. 'I'm sorry I
brought back bad memories for you.'

'Don't be, it's not your fault. You didn't know. Bloody
lies.'

'You mentioned once that you didn't know about your
brother's existence until recently. What was that about?'

'My dad fathered Jett with another woman a few months
after he married my mum. He confessed to me on his
deathbed.'

'That's tough.'

'That's the poisonous nature of secrets and lies.'

He looked away towards the docks, then said, 'While
we're sort of on the subject, I don't think I mentioned
Sunny's going to be your new neighbour.'

'No, you sort of didn't. When did you plan on sort of
telling me?'

'I'm telling you now. The house is for her—she has a new job with Hope Strings starting soon.'

'Sunny's with Hope Strings? That's great.' But living next door, not so much. Could be awkward. 'I look forward to meeting her.'

'I think you two will get along well. You're like her in some respects.' He turned, his gaze brightening as if he'd had a light-bulb moment. 'She's impulsive and loves spontaneity. Like you. Do you have a valid passport?'

Huh? 'Yes, why?'

'Ever been to Singapore?'

'No, but—'

'I'm there next weekend on business. Forget Heaven. Come with me to the Gardens by the Bay.'

CHAPTER TEN

'I CAN'T JUST fly off to Singapore with you.' But the very idea was already whisking her off on a magic carpet of thrilling anticipation. 'I have clients, appointments. People depending on me.'

'Business-class flight, Marina Bay Sands hotel,' he told her. As if that would make a difference.

She'd spent too much of her life struggling for acceptance and building a good professional reputation to risk it by abandoning her clients when they needed her, particularly those suffering through cancer treatments, just to run off with a man.

But not just any man. This was Leo Hamilton, and he was flying her overseas for the weekend, business class, and staying in that famous hotel she'd only ever dreamed about with its infinity pool fifty-seven storeys high and... and...

The very spontaneity of the idea appealed to her on so many levels.

A once-in-a-lifetime opportunity for the ultimate dirty weekend. Or maybe it was a romantic getaway this time. Brie's mind whirled; her heart did a little tap dance inside her chest. 'I...'

'If you can juggle a few appointments on Friday, we'll leave in the afternoon, and return early Monday morn-

ing. You'll be back at Eve's before morning tea break.
Can that work? I—'

'Your proposal's accepted.'

Leo fought back a grin, relieved his powers of persua-
sion, at least, were still in good working order. 'That was
quick.' And the best answer he'd heard all morning.

He gestured to a nearby bin and they headed towards
it. He was still trying to figure out how he'd asked her to
accompany him as they walked across the grass. He'd always kept his private and business lives separate.

What was it about Breanna that had him changing lifelong habits? One look into her dark eyes and he knew. He
couldn't wait to get her naked and he was prepared to do
whatever it took to spend some quality uninterrupted time
with her. Even if it meant taking her on a business trip.
And if personal and business got a little tangled up, what
the hell was wrong with that?

Things could end up getting a little knotted.

He refused to examine that thought further. He'd made
his decision. Chucking their half-eaten pancakes in the bin,
he rocked back on his heels, tossed the end of his scarf
over his shoulder. 'Come home with me.'

'Home? As in West Wind?'

'Your place. My place. Who cares where?'

'Not West Wind. Because when it's over with us...' The
air was calm but she tightened her arms around herself as
if a cold gust had blown through her.

Yeah. He understood. And the knowledge, too, left him
with a lead-ball sensation behind his breastbone, which
was best dismissed. But he did know what they both
wanted right now. And West Wind was never going to be
an option for them. 'Where's the nearest hotel?'

'Hey.' Laughing, she tapped his chest. 'You *can* be
spontaneous.' Grabbing his hand, she pulled him along.
'This way. And it happens to be a five star.'

'As long as it has a bed.'

'Who needs a bed?' She laughed again. He could get used to that sound.

The desk manager didn't bat an eyelid when they arrived at the lobby desk breathless and without luggage and requested a room. But Leo saw a glimmer in the man's eyes as he handed him their room key.

Leo wanted to tell the man he'd never done this in his life, that it wasn't what it looked like. That he wasn't spending a quick couple of hours heating up the sheets with some stranger he'd just met; that she wasn't a hooker. But Breanna was already dragging him towards the elevator bank.

The moment she pressed the button, the elevator doors opened and she grinned at Leo, anticipation sparkling in her eyes. No one else was waiting and they stepped in.

'Hang o—' The rest of his words were cut off when she yanked him close, pressed her mouth to his before the lift doors had finished closing.

She tasted of spicy heat and wild honey and he struggled to remain upright when she pushed up against him, knocking them both against the back wall.

He spread his feet for balance and placed his hands on her arms to steady them both. Which put him at a disadvantage when she reached down between them, found him rock hard and ready for action. 'Brie.' He swallowed as heat spurted into his lower belly. 'Slow down!'

It was no laughing matter but Breanna's eyes lit with humour as she cupped her hands around him. Moulded, stroked, squeezed. 'One speed, Leo, and it ain't slow.'

'But we're in a public lift.'

'You think like a girl,' she told him, an echo of his words not long ago. 'You're way too conservative, Mr Hamilton. Way too uptight and...'

She squeezed him again and smiled against his lips, sending more sparks shooting straight to his groin. Wondering vaguely if he might spontaneously combust, he tightened his fingers on her arms, hauled her closer, heard her muffled moan of approval as he devoured her mouth once more.

He couldn't recall whether either of them had pressed the button for their floor. He hoped one of them had because this could end badly for them. Then the lift dinged, the doors slid open and somehow they made it to their room without getting arrested.

She was stripping off her jacket as she made her way to the floor-to-ceiling windows overlooking the wharves where a pale sun cast a lemony square over the room's thick white carpet.

Tugging off her jumper, yanking off her boots and peeling her jeans down her long toned legs, the shining waterfall of black hair sliding over her shoulders. She stood in the patch of sunlight wearing only a playful smile and a strawberry charm that winked cheekily in her belly button while he pulled his jumper over his head, dropped it on the bed. She looked like some tall and gorgeous genie who'd won a temporary reprieve from her bottle home and wanted to make the most of her brief freedom.

Then she went very still, her smile gone. 'What *is* that?'

Leo was used to the reaction. Breanna hadn't seen it the last time they'd had sex because he'd not taken the time to undress. But he didn't see revulsion in her eyes, just concern as she studied the ugly scar that puckered the right side of his body from waist to hip to the front of his thigh.

'It's nothing.'

'It's *something*. What happened?'

He shrugged, not wanting to talk about it. 'We didn't come here to trade war stories.' Even now, his father was still trying to rule his life from the grave.

No frigging way. He was stronger now. In control of

his circumstances. Able to look out for Sunny the way she deserved to be.

'I can see why you freaked out about my dumb fire accident.'

And he wanted to share his story with her. Only her. She could listen to his story and learn. 'There was a house fire. I escaped relatively unscathed, considering. Imagine this happening all over your body.' He remembered the sight so vividly it was an open wound that never healed. 'Imagine your body so charred no one can recognise you, not even your own son.

'Or imagine you suffer forty per cent burns, like my sister did, and you live. Permanently disabled, with pain a daily struggle. If only I could have got her out sooner. Now do you understand why I reacted the way I did?'

She reached out, her eyes moist, touching his scars. Touching his soul. 'Your mother? I'm so very sorry. How old were you?'

'Eighteen.'

'And you saved your sister's life,' she murmured in wonder.

'I'm no hero. Can we get back on track here?' He pulled her close, felt her naked flesh against his for the first time warm and close and soothing against his. He kissed her long and deep. He was alive.

Then he let her go and walked to the room's CD player, facing away from her. 'When I turn around I want all that stuff gone. Finished. Because I want to be inside you but I don't want to be inside you with my past coming between us.'

He remained that way a moment to settle them both, then switched the player on. Mellow sax floated out.

When he turned back she'd lowered herself to the carpet. She nodded. 'We're good.' Using her hands behind her head as a pillow, she spread herself out like a banquet of sugar and spicy delights and stared up at him, a smile on her lips. 'Come on down.'

His fingers were shaking as he shoved his jeans off and joined her on the floor, banging his knee on the leg of an armchair on the way. Swearing, he rolled onto his back. 'You got an aversion to beds?'

'No, they're great for sleeping.' His minor mishap had broken the tension and she laughed. From her supine position, she raised herself onto her elbows. 'Ouch. Want me to kiss that better for you?'

His pulse beat fast and harsh in his ears. 'Yeah, but it's not my knee that's hurting.'

'I know,' she said and shuffled up beside him, tapped his nose with a fingertip. 'Close your eyes.'

'I—'

'Remember that conversation? The one where I own the dance floor? And I'm not going to lie back and let you do all the work, so man up, Leo, and let me be me for you.'

'I never said…you assumed…' He trailed off, his whole body tightening as her intention became clear, and closed his eyes as requested.

He heard the soft *shoosh* of the room's air conditioning, a busker playing the bagpipes down at Salamanca, Brie's not-quite-steady breathing near his ear. He drew in the scent of her bare skin and struggled with the primitive urge to tumble her onto her back and finish it, but he'd given his word and he owed her.

Then warm lips were dropping a path of petal-soft kisses as she slithered over him, silky skin abrading his. Smooth hands, capable fingers, tracing his collarbones, circling his nipples. A harsh groan tore from his throat but she didn't stop.

Lower.

Lightly touching his scarred torso, running her fingers over his hip's damaged and knotted skin. His eyes snapped open. Just simple acceptance in hers. She smiled as she lowered her lips there, to kiss the puckered surface. 'It's your story here and it's a magnificent one,' she said. 'One of courage and sacrifice.'

Leo thought he nodded but his eyes blurred and he closed them again so she wouldn't see a man reduced to the humiliation of something close to tears by a woman's tender words and understanding touch.

Lower.

Mindless mayhem, drugging delights. 'Breanna,' he gritted through his teeth, filling his greedy, restless hands with her hair, twisting and bunching the silky strands in his fists. Taking him far away from the ugliness.

And as she shot him skyward with her mouth and tongue, teeth and hands, every dark fantasy he'd had about her faded in the brilliance of the real thing.

Then just when he thought he couldn't last another second, she rose up, straddled herself over him and sank slowly down his length. Tight, hot, wet. He opened his eyes to watch. Her heavy breasts hung free, hair in disarray around her shoulders, the black ends caressing her olive skin and wine-dark nipples.

Their gazes tangled, reflected, entwined. Neither spoke in that breathless hiatus. Neither moved.

The earth stopped turning. Or maybe it spun out of its orbit—he didn't know—but he *did* know in that skipped heartbeat his world changed forever.

Brie saw the instant his eyes changed. Darkened, deepened. She told herself it was a shifting of the light, a cloud drifting over the sun, that she was imagining it. But she couldn't seem to get her breath; her heart felt swollen, too big for her chest.

Simple seduction was no longer the only thing happening in this convenient hotel room. Not after he'd shared his story. They were bonded in some inexplicable way. She knew there were other forces fuelling their passion as she began to move. Slowly. Over him, with him, for him, their movements in perfect sync, as if he'd been made for her at some exclusive Tiffany's in the sky.

Their fast demands and desperation yielded to something that flowed slower, richer, stronger. Something that came with consequences because the parameters of their relationship had shifted forever.

She knew she couldn't allow it, that she'd have to end it and move on, but right now she'd never felt more free, more alive. *Live in the moment,* she reminded herself as they crested the wave, tumbled over the other side and slid into a lazy fulfilment.

Moments later, side by side, they lay staring at the foam-speckled soundproofing on the ceiling. What had happened wasn't supposed to have happened. Not the sex—the other thing. But she couldn't walk away from this amazing connection yet. Not yet.

She exhaled slowly, her body still throbbing, her mind reeling. It took a monumental effort to keep it casual, the way she wanted it. The way she knew he wanted it. 'I know I said I wanted post-coital conversation, but I think we just said it all with that performance.'

'What did we say?' He spoke with care, as if worried what she meant.

'You're good. We're good. Shall we get going?'

'What's the rush?' He traced a tempting finger over her breasts and she very nearly changed her mind.

'You're not a woman, you wouldn't understand.' She rose, grabbing items of clothing and dragging them on, needing to be gone *now.* Before she had time to *think.*

'I need to find my passport at some stage…' She trailed off as his hand wrapped around her ankle then shook her head and moved away with a mountain of regret to tug on her boots. 'You've seen the state of my house. Some stuff's

there, some's at Jett's place.' She gave a half-laugh. 'Lo-
cating it could take a while.'

'You want me to check West Wind?'

She felt a little shiver at the thought of him checking
out her underwear drawer. Some things were simply too
private. 'If you could just look in the living room and
kitchen? And my home office is next to the bedroom, the
key's in the top drawer of the kitchen dresser. I'll search
the rest if you don't find it.'

'You locked me out?'

Reassured at his almost wounded expression, she
smiled. He'd never tried to gain entry to the rooms she'd
told him were private. Kudos to him. It meant a lot that she
could trust him. 'That was before. I know you better now.'

In the early hours of Thursday morning, Leo was still
awake. In Breanna's bed in West Wind trying not to notice
her lingering perfume, which he couldn't seem to eradi-
cate from his nostrils.

Breanna. He'd tried consistently but he didn't think he'd
ever get used to calling her Brie. Yet the casual name suited
her personality so well. When he was intimate with her,
or thinking intimate thoughts, which was ninety-nine per
cent of the time, she was Brie. Perhaps that was why he
preferred to use Breanna when interacting with her at other
times? It was more formal, one step removed. Maintaining an emotional distance.

You sure about that distance, Leonardo?

His mind spun back to the hotel. In that life-changing
moment when his emotions had been all over the shop.
She was different from anyone he'd ever met and he didn't
seem to know how to be himself around her. She wasn't
like other women he knew who gushed over receiving
flowers. Now he knew why. And who else would argue
over the free installation of a fire alarm?

He wasn't used to independent, confident women. He didn't understand them. The kind of women he'd dated had never done a striptease in front of a wall of windows in the glare of full sunlight. They'd never tried to seduce him in a lift.

Most hadn't acknowledged his scars, preferring to ignore them altogether than ask the awkward questions. He'd seen distaste in the eyes of some who had. Not Breanna. She'd embraced them as a part of who he was, and wasn't that refreshing?

None of those women knew his story. None had ever tugged on his heartstrings. Shoving back the quilt, he stalked to the window and stared at East Wind, silhouetted against the night sky. *Heartstrings?* That was new.

But then he'd never been with a woman like Breanna Black.

Brie.

The instant he'd caught sight of her last Saturday after just a few days of not seeing her, he'd realised how much he'd missed her sassiness, her directness. You knew where you stood with her. If she didn't like something, you knew about it. For a mad moment, he'd had this crazy notion that he could get used to seeing her every day.

Was it so crazy?

On an oath he swung away, headed downstairs for a glass of water. Time to think seriously about what she meant to him. How she might fit into his life.

Brie.

Busy, energetic and professional. She put others' needs before her own. But the tornado-swept room she called her home office, her living spaces, which should be havens of relaxation: all total chaos. Anathema to him. Gulping water, he started upstairs once more. He sincerely hoped she found her passport.

Brie.

Hopelessly disorganised.

He'd searched where she'd asked, without success. In the meantime, he'd reorganised her garden shed and purchased a palm for the front veranda and a few exotic herbs missing from her collection. The least he could do to repay her for the convenience of allowing him to stay here. He'd made a start on sorting her library but decided to postpone. He could be overstepping the mark.

All of which had left him seriously behind schedule.

On Thursday afternoon, Leo was at Breanna's dining-room table still finishing the project report he needed to take with him before they left the country tomorrow afternoon. He'd never been so disorganised before an important business meeting.

After last night's soul-searching he'd spent the morning relocating his gear to East Wind. The renovations had been finished for a few days but he'd dragged his feet moving back, telling himself he had too much work to catch up on. Plus he'd been to Freycinet then on to Launceston to meet with clients.

Now, he knew, it was time; too much had changed between them. With Sunny's furniture not here yet, he'd sleep on the floor when they returned from Singapore. Preferable to lying awake in Breanna's bed with nothing to do but think.

His heart skipped a beat when her personalised chime sounded on his mobile. 'Breanna. How's—?'

'I can't find my passport.'

'Are you serious?'

'I've been to West Wind while you were away like I told you—just very quickly, to search my room. I didn't snoop through your stuff, bu—'

'I know you didn't snoop, Breanna.' He drummed his fingers on the dining table. 'You've left it till twenty-four hours before we leave to inform me you still haven't found your passport?'

'You said you'd be busy. I didn't want to bother you with my little problem. And I was packing,' she said, defensive. 'I have to dress to impress. What if one of your important colleagues sees me? I think I'll get a new bikini…'

'*Little* problem?' He rubbed a hand over gritty eyes. To erase the swimsuit image or was it frustration with her skewed priorities? 'You don't need to wear anything but skin to impress me and you won't be meeting my colleagues, so stop with the packing and start with the hunting. Have you any idea where you saw it last?'

'So you hide your dates from your colleagues?'

'We were talking about your passport?'

'I haven't used it since I went to Bali three years ago.'

'Breanna.' He rolled his gaze to the ceiling. How could he have even contemplated being involved with such a disorganised person? 'Do you want me to look anywhere else?'

'Would you? I'm pretty sure now that it's in the kitchen. I had this flash—'

He hit Save and pushed back his chair. 'I scoured the kitchen.'

'Have you checked the biscuit barrel with the fifties girl picture on the front? The brunette in the spotty dress? Top shelf right up high next to the fridge.'

He snapped his fingers. 'Now why didn't I think of that?'

CHAPTER ELEVEN

BRIE DANGLED HER legs over the edge of the opulent Marina Bay Sands Hotel's infinity pool and watched the early morning sun paint Singapore's unique skyscrapers pink and gold.

She wriggled her toes in the water while she admired her tropical-print bikini, newly purchased from the Skypark shop. Leo had left for his meeting thirty minutes ago. The poor guy had looked whacked this morning. She grinned to herself—probably because they'd not reached their room till just before one a.m. after the long flight. It was now seven-thirty and they'd put those few hours to good use. Not a lot of sleeping had been involved.

She'd zoned out for most of the journey in her spacious business-class seat whereas Leo had been working like a fever on his laptop. So she was super refreshed and ready to hit The Shoppes at the bottom of the spectacular structure as soon as she'd eaten what promised to be a delicious breakfast in one of the restaurants conveniently close to the pool.

The morning passed too quickly: a frivolous shopping spree, a thirty-minute massage, morning tea in a speciality chocolate café.

At two p.m. Leo met her in the lobby and they were chauffeured by limo to the famous Raffles Hotel with its attractive British architecture. They enjoyed the Tiffin

Room's curry buffet sitting at one of the black lacquered bamboo tables and swapping stories about their respective mornings.

After lunch Leo enjoyed showing Breanna the stunning Gardens by the Bay. They wandered through the two conservatories—climate-controlled biomes aptly named the Flower Dome and the Cloud Forest.

He explained to his rapt audience of one that a sustainable feature was the horticultural waste generated within the Flower Dome, which in turn generated electricity to maintain its cool, temperate mini-climate.

Then they took an open-air vehicle to the solar-powered Supertrees nearby. He'd visited the vertical gardens half a dozen times and their other-worldly beauty still captured his enthusiasm and imagination. Today was a bonus; he was sharing it with a first-time visitor who obviously enjoyed it as much as he.

'Amazing, aren't they?' She turned a circle gazing up at the impressive steel structures covered in ferns and tropical blooms. 'They remind me of that movie, Avatar.'

'Yes, they are a bit Pandora-like.' He took her hand. 'There's a spectacular view from the skywalk.'

'So what's your professional interest in them?' she asked as they viewed the Bay Gardens from the sky bridge connecting some of the fifty-metre-high structures.

He explained how they mimicked real trees by harnessing solar energy, which was used for their attractive lighting, and how rainwater was collected for irrigation and water displays. 'My business colleagues and I are working on a plan for something similar in Australia. Probably somewhere along Sydney Harbour or nearby.'

He filled her in on his meeting with his Singaporean counterparts. Their combined plan to create similar structures in Australia within the next five years. His particular expertise in this innovative and specialised field was somewhat unique—he'd put forward a bold initiative for the Aussie Outback, which had been received with cautious optimism.

They stopped to buy ice creams. When had he talked about his business life with anyone beyond the occasional colleague? He'd discussed aspects with Sunny, but only when she'd asked, which wasn't often since she said getting info from him was as painful as chopping off her violinist's fingers one by one with a rusty blade.

He worked alone and liked it that way. But he found sharing his work with Breanna, seeing the genuine interest in her lively eyes, and answering her intelligent questions, a rewarding and energising experience. Almost as good as sex. He remembered last night's marathon—the way she'd unravelled beneath him—and smiled to himself. Almost as good but not quite.

'What's going on in there?' She tapped his temple, a sultry look in her midnight eyes. 'It's obviously wicked and debauched.'

'Wildly.' He pressed his lips to her forehead, tasted her skin's salty glow. 'Far too wicked to tell you in public.'

'So let's go back to our room and we can have Show and Tell.' She shifted against him in the growing dimness. 'I can't wait.'

'Soon.' He took her hand, tugged her close so that her hard little nipples grazed his shirt, an appetiser before the main course later. 'I want you to see the light and sound show first.'

'We'll make our own,' she murmured against his ear.

Sensitive body parts constricted at the husky promise. 'I'm counting on it.'

As dusk came, the trees' solar lights began to glimmer like colourful glow-worms, then the featured show lit up the sky. The audience oohed and aahed. Leo preferred to watch the rainbow reflections playing over Breanna's animated face.

Afterwards, he wined and dined her at Boat Quay, a vibrant open-air restaurant strip along the Singapore River that reminded him of Sydney's bustling Darling Harbour.

When they at last stepped into their suite, Brie entered first and left the lights off. She set her handbag down on her way to admire the night view, her eyes drifting inevitably to the king-sized bed as she passed.

It seemed an age since she'd left those rumpled sheets that smelled of sweet sin this morning. In other ways, it seemed like a minute, and the minutes were ticking away. This was their last night here. *Better make the most of it.* The bed was now as smooth as a lake, the edge of the crisp white sheet folded down in invitation, butter-coloured Singapore orchids on the pillow.

In the dimness, she stripped off her clothes where she stood. She walked to the full-length sliding doors that led to their balcony, which was bedecked with a profusion of purple bougainvillaea. Singapore's cityscape of lights dazzled.

'Brie.' Leo's voice was close but not intimately so, even though he was using her shortened name—which seemed to stick in his throat. She could see his reflection over her shoulder.

'Don't turn around,' he said, so quickly that she barely picked up on the thread of tension tightening his vocal chords.

'This trip's been amazing,' he said. 'You've been amazing. You *are* amazing.'

She watched in astonishment as he slid something heavy around her neck. A necklace. And not just any necklace. Tiny rainbows twinkled on her décolletage. She'd have sworn he'd stolen it from some royal collection except that this wasn't ornate and overdone. It was a modern asymmetrical design in gold with a row of diamonds along one edge. Simple yet striking. Astonishment swiftly turned to panic.

Oh. No. 'What have you done?' Shaking her head, she turned to him, flung her hands in the air. 'What does this mean?'

'That I… That I'd like to keep seeing you when we get back.'

'What do you mean? I don't understand what you mean by that.' Her voice rose a couple of notches as she fought the conflicting emotions twisting like razor ribbons inside her. 'Or this.' She lifted the heavy gold away from her skin, felt the runaway pulse at her neck as she did so.

'It means I'd like us to be more. It means I want to explore us further and see where it leads.'

Her heart turned over, her blood ran hot then cold. She couldn't look at him and turned away. 'I thought we wanted the same thing. A no-strings kind of thing. A fun kind of thing. We agreed that day in my office, remember? You looked horrified with the notion that it should be anything other than just sex.'

'Who says we can't change our minds?' he said behind her.

'You've changed your mind?' She stared at his reflection behind her. He'd changed his mind. 'Oh my *God*…' She shoved at the balcony door so she wouldn't see his reflection and it slid open silently. She barely noticed the clammy evening air on her naked skin. All she could feel was the necklace's heavy weight. *The String*. 'I thought you understood already—I'm not like other women. I don't *want* gifts.'

'What *do* you want, Breanna?'

It hurt, irrationally so, that he'd reverted to the safety of his formality. Cool, *displeased* formality. 'I want us to continue the way we have been.'

'And we can,' he assured her. 'I'm not talking marriage

and everlasting, I'm simply suggesting a more stable ongoing arrangement. A more exclusive arrangement.'

His last words chilled her. Just like the boys back in her teens who assumed… She spun to face him. 'I *don't* sleep around. I already told you: if I'm sleeping with a guy, he's the only guy I'm sleeping with. And I expect the same from that guy.'

'I crossed that possibility off the list a long time ago, baby doll.'

'There you go again—*baby doll*? For heaven's sakes, I'm hardly petite.' To divert the topic of old prejudices, she reached deep down inside for aggravation.

'What I meant was I want *you* to feel you can trust *me* to be exclusive. Don't take it off,' he said, when she reached behind for the necklace's clasp.

'It was a no-strings deal.' She lifted the gold away from her skin. 'You do realise this is a *string* in our no-strings agreement, don't you?'

His brows lifted in genuine surprise. 'It's no such thing. Calm down. We can keep it as simple as you want.'

She did as he requested and left The String alone because she didn't want to spoil this night and, judging by his response, maybe she *was* overreacting. He'd just promised to keep it as simple as she wanted. 'I don't need a pet name. Unless it's Brie.'

'You're still a shorty to me. *Brie*. And we'll do this however you want, so don't stress.'

Her smile came slowly at the reassurance in his voice and the laughter lines crinkling around his eyes; she was relieved they seemed to be on track once more. 'There'll be no stressing tonight,' she promised him. 'And maybe I am petite after all coz you're the tallest man I've ever been with.'

'And you're the tallest woman I've been with. But you're

still a shorty.' He patted her head. 'With me you'll always be a shorty.'

With me. Always. The words rolled off his tongue as if he meant forever and was totally comfortable with it. As if he'd made up his mind and expected her to fall in with his decisions.

She didn't want forever. She wanted freedom. She wanted to leave her options open in case... In case. *No heart, no hurt.*

But forever was no closer, no more substantial than hopes and wishes. *Now* was in her grasp. She could feel it. *Now* surrounded her, the way Leo surrounded her. His scent, his touch, the sound of his quickened breathing near her ear.

And for now, for once, she'd forget he'd tried to change the rules they'd agreed to play by. She lifted her arms around his neck and clung tight. 'For tonight, can we just be lovers?'

Leo thought he heard an edge of desperation to her plea. In answer, he hauled her naked body flush against him. He filled his hands with her breasts while he nuzzled behind her ear and murmured, 'Where do you want me to start?'

'Right there's just fine,' she breathed. 'And make it slow, make it last, you're so good at that.'

He smiled into her hair. Damned if he understood this perplexing woman, but at least he knew what she wanted in the bedroom. She smelled of sweet tropical blooms and midnight and he set about filling her request to the best of his ability.

They landed in Sydney at seven-thirty on Monday morning. Once through Customs, Brie was continuing to Hobart without Leo. Seemed he had a connecting flight to Melbourne that he'd neglected to tell her about.

'So when will you be back in Hobart?' she asked as they manoeuvred their luggage towards the taxi stand.

'A couple of days. I need to help Sunny pack and since I've not heard back from her...' mini hesitation—unusual for a man who was always in charge of everything and everyone '...I want to check everything's on schedule.' Swinging his cabin bag over his shoulder, he opened a taxi door for her. 'Any plans for this week?'

'Apart from working my butt off to make up for lost time?'

His smile was fleeting. 'I meant evenings.'

She knew that. It was time to pull back; she needed breathing space. Just space. 'A charity event and three parties.' She didn't know who was socialising yet but she'd find them. She always did. 'I'll need tonight off to find Party Babe Brie—she's been MIA lately. Oh...' She pulled out The String tucked inside its velvet box, held it out. 'I don't need gifts to remember what a wonderful time I had, but I do appreciate the sentiment behind it.'

His whole body tightened, stiffened.

Brutally offended.

'Do what you want with it. Sell it. Or auction it for your charity.'

She didn't need to see his eyes behind his sunglasses to read his emotions in his body language and tone of voice and she wanted to weep and rage with frustration. She knew no sane woman would have refused such a gift. He still didn't get it—still didn't understand that she wasn't like other women. And right now, a little *in*sane.

Did he still not realise he'd broken the rules of their agreement? 'Leo...' she ventured, then paused, lost for words.

'You getting in, buddy?' she heard the cabbie ask.

Leo shook his head once. 'Domestic terminal for the lady, please,' he said. And pushed the door shut.

* * *

Leo opened the front door of his Melbourne home an hour later to discover the entire hallway lined with packing boxes, sealed and ready for transportation.

He dumped his cabin bag at his feet and bellowed, 'Sunny!' And instantly regretted his lapse. Given their shared pasts any show of temper towards his sister was an unforgivable sin. He'd seen what damage runaway emotions could do by watching his father.

But today something tore free and wouldn't be leashed. 'What's going on?'

'Leo. Hi.' She came out of the lounge. 'I was—'

He swept a hand over her belongings. 'I told you to wait.'

'Didn't need to.' Her awkward gait was more pronounced today as she moved towards him on her crutch.

He wanted to hit something but curled his fists instead. 'Overdoing it as usual, Miss Independent?'

She blinked, but to her credit she didn't react to his outburst. 'Not at all,' she said. 'I'm fine. I'm not sure about you though.'

'You didn't return my call.' Dammit, he *wanted* an argument from her.

'A friend helped me. I knew you were busy and I wanted to get it done.' She looked up at him, concern in her blue eyes. 'Weekend didn't go well?'

He waved it off. He didn't want to talk about the weekend. He'd told her he was going to Singapore for business and might have mentioned he might take a friend along. A mistake to tell her. Bigger mistake to have tried to combine business with pleasure. He focused on the more immediate concern. 'It appears you're ready to leave.'

'The moving van should be here any minute.'

'You were going to leave without telling me.' Something twisted inside him. She really was branching out into the world on her own. He wanted to put his arms around her and protect her as he'd always done but she didn't need him any more—hadn't for some time. He'd chosen not to notice but now the reality was staring him in the face, literally.

'No, Leo. Of course not,' she soothed. 'The stuff's going but I'm catching tomorrow afternoon's flight. I couldn't leave without sharing a last supper with my favourite brother. You will be here tonight, won't you? Mrs J's making our favourite dumpling stew.'

He breathed out slowly. 'I'll be here. Tell me your flight details, I've got a meeting in the city tomorrow afternoon but I'll change it and come back when I've got you settled in.'

'Leo. I'm flying down with a friend from the new orchestra,' she said gently. 'I'm staying with him until my stuff arrives. At least a week or two.'

Leo felt as if he'd turned to stone. *'He.'* He watched her wait for some sign of support from him, but he knew it wouldn't make a difference. She didn't need his permission or his approval. 'Gregor Goldsworthy.'

'He'll take good care of me.'

Suck it up, big brother, and say nothing *to dim that smile on her face.* 'Make sure he does or he'll answer to me.'

Her smile widened, reaching her sparkling blue eyes. 'It's a good feeling knowing I have my brother at my back if I need him.'

If she needed him. Something brighter burned in her eyes, he noticed now, and it tore at something deep. Big changes were coming. He felt as if everything was slipping away from him. 'Why the sudden decision to leave now?'

'You said the renovation was finished. I decided to move straight away so you'll have this place to yourself.' She smiled. 'That way you won't have to sneak around any more when you want to bring someone home with you.'

The only person he wanted to bring home was Brie.

'I've had to put my stuff in East Wind for a bit, so it could be a case of reversed situations. I've taken a spare room and in the meantime I promise to stay out of your way.'

'What happened to the arrangement with...Breanna, isn't it?'

'Wasn't working out.'

'Aah.' A woman's knowing eyes focused on him, which was odd, since they were his little sister's eyes. 'So Breanna's the mystery girl who's had you tied up in knots.' Her smile sobered; her blue eyes sympathised. 'What happened?'

He shrugged, his shoulders tense. 'No mystery. I took her out a couple of times. So what?'

'So Singapore's no ordinary date, that's what.'

'I didn't...' He leaned a tight shoulder against the wall. He'd never slide this one past Sunny. Defeat—it felt a lot like defeat, and it was an unfamiliar sensation. But she was the only person he'd ever confided in. 'If someone gave you a diamond necklace,' he said slowly, 'what would you do?'

'Diamonds.' She tapped her chin, her eyes searching his. 'That's serious bling.'

'No.' He waved a dismissive hand. 'It was just a souvenir. Token. Something simple. How would you receive it? And don't overanalyse.'

'It would depend on who he was and how we defined our relationship.'

There she went, all deep and meaningful again. He shook his head. 'Forget it, it's not important.'

'Are you talking about the relationship or the diamonds?'

'Neither. Both.' Hell. 'A simple answer without the psychobabble would have sufficed.'

He turned on his heel but she reached out with her crutch, tapped his arm, forcing him to turn back. 'You didn't let me finish. If I wasn't sure where I stood with the guy concerned, or where the relationship was headed, or even if I thought we might want different things from such a relationship, I might be wary of accepting such a gift.'

Considering, he scratched his bristled jaw. Had he got too intense too soon? Was Brie simply being cautious? Or was she guarded and hiding how she really felt behind that nonchalant attitude she was so good at because she was afraid?

For a guy who dated often, he was clueless about this particular woman who was the polar opposite of the sort he was accustomed to. 'Thanks.' He lifted a finger. 'If this *friend* of yours—the one whose home you're going to be staying in—if he gave you a…token of his…' He lifted a hand, dropped it.

'I'd say thank you and wear it with love.'

'Love?'

She nodded and something burned in her eyes.

He turned, muttered, 'Let me get used to it,' and headed back the way he'd come.

'It's okay to show you care, Leo,' Sunny said behind him. 'Whether it works out the way you want it to or not, expressing your feelings—however you do that—is not a weakness. When are you going to get that through that stubborn head of yours?'

CHAPTER TWELVE

BRIE WAS EXTREMELY busy the first couple of days after their return. She was grateful for it. But the evenings were a different story. Solo and filled with the fast clack of her knitting needles rather than party sounds. Chamomile tea instead of red wine.

She hadn't even wanted Sam's company. Or maybe she didn't want to foist her poor humour onto her friend.

She'd returned to West Wind as soon as she'd read Leo's brief text explaining he'd moved out. No matter how spacious and elegant and modern the retreat was, West Wind was home and she'd missed it. Its solitude and class. The smell of fresh pine cones in the fireplace. The wind song through the row of pencil pines that divided the two homes. There was something so comforting about the familiar.

She couldn't believe what he'd done with her garden shed. Everything tidy and sorted and shelved from empty pots to fertiliser to tools. Plastic labels on those shelves. A pretty sign on the inside of the door: *A place for everything and everything in its place.* Was he *serious*?

Why would he go to those lengths for her?

The more she thought about it, the faster her needles clacked. It was another kind of String. She'd be indebted to him for taking time out of his busy schedule and away from all those other people depending on his vast experience. She'd be obliged to thank him in some way for his kindness and generosity—which wasn't the problem—except that she hadn't asked for his help.

She was independent by choice. Free. Unencumbered. Uncommitted. And she loved it that way. She *did*.

Tossing her knitting down, she stood, flexing cramped fingers. Without words, Leo was saying she didn't know what she was doing in any aspect of her life and needed him to help her out of her mess. That he was just the man for the job.

Leo was trying to change her into someone she wasn't. Someone she didn't want to be. He'd stripped her naked in more ways than one and exposed her shortcomings and insecurities.

She swiped up the radio's remote, aimed and pressed, but she found the music's happy beat irritating and switched it off. Where was Party Babe Brie when she needed her distraction? No one distracted Brie better than her party persona and yet she seemed to have disappeared.

He'd made her lie.

The truth? Leo Hamilton was a good man. A dependable, responsible, kind, caring, generous, witty, sexy, clever, creative and amazing man.

He was just bad for her.

Leo had an appointment in country Victoria on Tuesday, and back-to-back meetings in Melbourne's CBD, on Wednesday, so he didn't make it back to Hobart until late Wednesday evening.

He lay on his inflatable mattress in the dark. He could've stayed in a hotel for the night but he'd wanted to check on East Wind. And he'd wanted to be close to West Wind.

His usual evening leisure activities hadn't worked for him in Melbourne; they weren't working here. Since returning from Singapore, no amount of reading or killer

Sudokus—not even Sunny's enchanting violin CD—could prevent his thoughts from wandering to Brie.

Because things had been up in the air and awkward when they'd said goodbye at Sydney airport, he'd sent her a text message to say he'd moved out of her place and into East Wind and left her a note advising her of same on her kitchen table. He still had her spare set of house keys.

He'd had a brief text reply thanking him for letting her know and for an 'amazing weekend'. Not another word about what was happening between them or any suggestion they get together soon. Nothing.

At least she'd replied. He told himself she was busy with rescheduled clients and her hectic social life.

Right.

Staring at the ceiling, he wondered, was she doing her party thing with another guy tonight?

If I'm sleeping with a guy, he's the only guy I'm sleeping with.

If there was one thing Leo knew about this woman it was that Brie did not lie.

Tonight the hushed still of the night and his solitude were all he had. He'd always been content with that. Until he'd met Brie and she'd worked her way under his skin like a prickle, then an itch.

Then all the way right into his heart.

He rubbed a fist over the place where on cue it throbbed and burned and ached.

Flinging back his quilt, he pushed up and stalked to the window and stared at West Wind's darkened windows. He shook his head, refusing to acknowledge the only possible reason why his entire chest felt as if it were caught in a vice. It couldn't be.

She wasn't his type. She wasn't anyone's type—she was unique. She was Brie.

Strong and smart and sexy. Messy. Honest and open

with a wicked sense of humour. A woman whose company inspired and entertained him. A whirlwind and a challenge. A woman he never tired of gazing at or sparring with or making love to.

Because love was exactly what he felt when they were together. When he buried himself inside her and held her close, looked into her bottomless black eyes. And denied it every time.

Not any more.

He tried on the word for size. 'Love...' The murmur felt foreign on his tongue but it fitted. With Brie, it fitted.

It was as if Sunny's words had unlocked something inside him. Freed him to examine his thoughts and emotions in a different way. And it didn't make him feel weak—he felt strong, invincible. A Superman.

Pulling on a T-shirt and jeans, he let himself out into the chilly air and headed to West Wind to wait for Brie. Whatever time she came home, he intended to be there. To tell her how he felt.

As he walked up the path to the front door, a slant of light coming from the room she liked to call The Parlour on the far side of the house caught his attention.

He walked along the path in that direction to check if her car was in the garage or if she'd been picked up, glancing in the window to check if everything was in order in the room on his way past.

Through the gauzy curtain, he saw Brie sitting on the overstuffed couch, hunched over as if in pain, the heels of her hands pressed to her brow.

Was she ill? Not wanting to give her a heart attack by knocking on the pane, he jogged to the front door, let himself in with his keys, calling her name as he headed down the passage.

'Brie...' He stopped in the doorway. The scene was

not the scene he'd viewed through the window less than thirty seconds ago.

Surrounded by a sea of natural yarn, she looked up at him, all casual composure. So, the outward calm she presented wasn't always the way she felt inside.

She picked up a ball of driftwood-coloured wool and said, 'I thought you'd moved out?'

'I thought you were ill.'

'I'm perfectly well, as you can see.'

As he came further into the room, he could see her eyes were red and swollen. 'Not from where I'm standing.'

She didn't answer him, knotting the end of the wool in her hand to the charcoal yarn and picking up a pair of lethal-looking knitting needles he'd not noticed earlier.

'That's going to be some scarf when it's done.' He moved closer, willing her to look at him, but she lowered her head to her work. 'You made it abundantly clear your social calendar was chock-a-block this week,' he said. 'You've accused me of making assumptions, so I'm going to ask you to tell me if I've got it wrong in assuming you told me that to avoid seeing me.'

Her head bent further, her hands faltered and she nodded.

She might as well have plunged her knitting needles into his chest because they wouldn't have hurt as much as the pain that arced through his heart. 'Why?'

Setting her knitting aside, she shook her head. 'This. Us.' She made a to-and-fro movement between them with her hands. 'It's better to end it now.'

'Why?' He heard the curt demand in his voice, reined himself in, tried again, calmer this time though his insides were cramping and everything was unravelling like her wool. 'Can I ask why?'

'You rearranged my garden shed.'

What? 'Yes. But—'

'You don't get it, do you?' She lifted devastated eyes to his. 'When someone just comes in and takes it on himself to change everything. When someone tries to reorder my life?'

'Your *garden shed*,' he corrected. 'Or are you talking about something else?'

She shook her head. 'I *like* messy. I'm comfortable with messy—it's who I am.' She rose, pinned him with an accusing look. 'I bet you arrange your DVDs in alphabetical order and woe betide anyone who forgets to put them back in their correct niches.'

'Chronological, actually.' He tried a smile but his lips wouldn't cooperate. 'What else? Surely one mistake on my part can't have changed your mind.'

'Your grand gestures.' She ground a fist into her open palm against her chest. 'Flowers, diamonds. I don't need them. Don't want them.'

'Is it a crime to want to show a person I appreciate her?'

'So it makes *you* feel good?'

'Wrong.' But he thought of other times with other women when it had been exactly that. It was different with Brie. 'You want me to go away—is that what you're trying to tell me?'

'I don't need a regular man in my life. I'm happy the way I am. Freedom's what I want.'

To his surprise—and hers, apparently—her eyes filled with tears.

'So why are you crying?'

'I'm not crying.' She swiped at her cheeks, swore under her breath. 'Okay, I'm crying.'

'You lied to me about your activities this week. The one person I trusted not to lie.'

'That's why you're bad for me.'

'I don't understand.'

'You took it upon yourself and changed the terms of our

relationship without giving me a say. You always have to be the boss; you can't let others make their own choices.'

'That's who I am.'

'A control freak's who you are.'

The truth of her words, unfair, struck at his core and anger simmered just below the surface. 'Let me tell you about control. My entire life was dictated by my father's actions. He'd turn up on Mum's pay day and take our rent money then disappear for weeks till the cash ran out. When I was old enough I took an after-school job to help.

'I was eighteen when I came home after work one night to find the bastard laying into her. When I intervened, he goaded me into swinging a punch and I just lost it. For the first time in my life I let the man get the better of me. I think I broke his nose. And it felt so friggin' good. So well deserved.'

Brie's swollen eyes filled with moisture. 'Leo…it's—'

'I'm not done.' Leo slashed the space between them with his hand. 'He left off Mum and staggered out like the coward he was. Great—I was prepared to do it again. Whatever it took to get him away from us.'

'That w—'

'I was wrong. He came back later that night when we were asleep and set fire to the place. *Because I lost control.*'

'*No.*'

She rose from the couch, reached a hand towards him but he held up a hand. 'Not now.'

Her arm fell to her side. 'You were protecting the ones you love.' Her voice was barely audible. 'Where is he now?'

'Dead. Killed by the fire he started.'

'I'm sorry,' she whispered. 'I shouldn't h—'

'I've cared for Sunny ever since. After surgery and physio and counsellors, she needed someone there for her, someone to make the decisions. In the absence of any other family, that person was me and I won't apologise for that.'

'I'm not asking for apologies.'

'So what are you asking for?' He narrowed his eyes, searching for some clue. 'Or are you too afraid to risk asking the question?'

What little colour she had drained from her face, leaving her chalk-white. Hugging defensive arms to her chest, she turned away from him, paced to the end of the sofa. 'It's better if you leave.'

'Better for who, Brie? You're not the woman you show to the world.' He waved a hand at her craftwork. 'Hiding away here after you made sure I thought you were out socialising this week.'

'I—'

'You're not only lying to me, you're lying to yourself. And that's the real tragedy.' He moved closer—one small step for a man. He saw fear in her eyes, and pain as she backed away further. 'You don't have to be afraid, Brie. Trust m—'

'Please. Just go. Go now.'

The finality in her plea hit him full force and he turned to do just that. But he stopped at the doorway. He wasn't leaving without saying what he'd come here to say. 'So you want to toss what we have away before we find out where it goes?'

'You're a very special man, Leo Hamilton, and it's been an amazing ride. But I like my freedom more.'

Freedom. A bitter laugh rose up his throat at the irony. How many times had he told himself he wanted the same? 'I came here tonight to wait for you to come home, no matter how long it took. To tell you I'm in love with you, and want you in my life permanently. I want it all. With you. The real kicker is that Sunny told me to lay my feelings for you on the line and just go for it.'

She stared at him, aghast, as if he had some contagious fatal disease. 'You can't be in love with me.'

'Why the hell not? I'll be the judge of who I'm in love with.'

'No.' The word fell from parched lips. 'Even if that were true, sooner or later you'll fall out of love and leave—emotionally if not physically. And that's the very worst kind of absence. The kind that drains your essence, drop by drop until there's nothing left but a shell.'

'Is that what Elliot did? Your parents?' The agony he saw in her eyes slayed him but she was measuring him against others. 'I'm not like that. What's more you *know* I'm not like that. One attribute I do have is stickability—ask Sunny. You're not being fair to me. To us.'

She wasn't listening to him, her gaze focused inwards. 'It's emotional abandonment,' she said, her voice trembling. 'And I won't let it happen to me. Not again.' She buried her face in her hands.

'You mean you're not prepared to take a risk even after I've bared my heart and soul to you.'

'Can't,' she whispered. 'Won't.'

'Life's a risk. Stepping out the front door in the morning's a risk. Coming here tonight was a risk.' He tossed her set of house keys on the nearest chair. 'When you're ready to take that risk, let me know. But don't take too long about it. Life's not only a risk, it's also short.'

As soon as Brie heard the front door close, her legs gave way and she sank to the floor, curled up into a ball and rocked. The world had officially gone crazy.

She'd just listened to the saddest story she'd ever heard. How much more pain had he endured than her? She'd wanted to reach out to him in that moment but he'd pushed her away, mentally shut her out. Ten seconds later he'd done an about-turn and said he was in love with her. He wanted her in his life forever.

The man who only a few days ago had assured her they could keep things as simple as she wanted—which just went to show men didn't know what they wanted and were incapable of keeping their word.

Simple as falling in love? She coughed out a bitter laugh. She'd been falling down that slippery slope since that fateful evening at East Wind when she'd introduced herself to Mr Perfect. Falling, sliding, scrambling—to keep her feet on the ground, her head in control of her stupid heart that wanted what it couldn't have.

And ultimately failing.

Where Leo was concerned, *no heart, no hurt* wouldn't work. She'd known that from the start. But Brie the Great Pretender had gone ahead and played her game of *let's stick to casual fun because I'm too afraid to trust anything deeper* anyway. And now she was going to pay the price for the rest of her life.

Because that was how long it would take to get over him.

A few weeks later, Brie glared at the catastrophe she called her salon's tiny office and flipped through another pile of miscellaneous papers strewn across her desk. A new client had made an appointment with Jodie only an hour ago and was due in ten minutes and Brie couldn't find the product order she'd printed out yesterday for the delivery guy who was turning up any minute now.

She could really do with Leo's organisational skills here.

The thought of Leo sent shards of pain shooting through her body for the fiftieth time this morning. He hadn't contacted her since that last horrible night. She could admit, now that it was too late to tell him, that she loved what he'd done with her garden shed. One day when things between them weren't so damaged—in a million years—

she'd let him know how much she appreciated his efforts. She pounced on the wayward paper beneath an empty takeaway coffee cup and headed to the shared reception area with it.

A young blonde woman with clear blue eyes stood at the desk. She leaned on an elbow crutch and smiled as Brie approached. There was something about that smile that reminded her of someone.

'Good morning.' Brie checked her new client's name on the information sheet Jodie handed her. 'Sky? Welcome. I'm Brie.' As she ushered Sky into her treatment room Brie noted beneath her black trousers one leg was deformed in some way. 'Have a seat and we'll have a quick chat.' She lit her Balinese Temple aromatherapy candles and switched on her calming CD. 'I see here you've chosen to try the chamomile and fruit facial and a hand massage?'

'Yes.' Sky set her crutch on the floor beside her.

Brie skimmed the form. 'You're from Primrose Bay.' A forty-minute drive away.

'I'm staying with a friend temporarily.'

Brie looked up. 'Not that I'm complaining, but why come all this way?'

'I looked up Eve's Naturally online. I like your use of natural products. Oh, and I admire what you're doing with Pink Snowflake, which you mentioned there too.' She smiled.

Brie smiled back. 'Let's get started, then.'

Brie always left it to her client to choose whether she wanted to talk or close her eyes and relax during treatments.

Sky was a talker. Brie asked the usual questions and answered Sky's responses on autopilot. But as usual, she couldn't seem to concentrate because she was thinking of Leo. How he was, what he was doing now, whether he'd found somewhere to live because she hadn't seen him near East Wind.

'Do you have a regular guy in your life?'

Brie heard the end of Sky's question and pulled herself back to the present. 'No.' She squirted lotion onto Sky's palm and worked it in with her thumb. 'You?'

'I do. We've been seeing each other for four months now. He's an amazing and gifted person.'

So is Leo. 'That's great.' Working her way up each of Sky's fingers in turn, Brie reminded herself she'd glimpsed what gave Sky that inner radiance and slammed the door on the possibility for herself.

Then Sky grimaced. 'I just wish my overprotective, control-freak brother thought so.'

'Some guys can be like that,' Brie said, thinking of one guy in particular. 'I'm sure your brother doesn't mean to be controlling.'

Sky coughed out a laugh. 'You reckon?'

'And dictatorial and overbearing too?' Brie suggested.

'Yeah.' Sky's smile turned wistful. 'But he's the best brother in the world and I wouldn't swap him for anything. Sometimes I forget to tell him.'

'I'm sure he knows. Maybe he's so focused on doing what he considers is in your best interests, he simply doesn't understand how he comes across.' Brie blinked at her own perceptiveness. 'Sorry,' she murmured. 'Enough of the psych talk.'

'Not at all. It's good to meet someone who understands. He's still getting used to the fact that I'm an adult now and want to do my own thing,' Sky went on. 'I think he just needs to be needed.' She cocked her head, bright eyes filled with interest. 'You've never had a guy in your life that you thought could be someone special?'

Brie's chest cramped while she squeezed and kneaded

Sky's hand, pressed deep into the palm. 'Yes. But I didn't want commitment. I wanted my freedom.'

'So is freedom still what you want or are you afraid of making the wrong decision?'

'I'm still thinking about that.' And why were Sky's questions so similar to those Leo had asked her? Those same questions she'd asked herself over and over since he'd walked out of her life.

'Men aren't good at expressing emotion,' Sky said. 'They don't want to talk about their feelings; they don't want to know about yours; it freaks them out and makes them feel like they've lost face somehow.'

'If they were more like women…'

'I'd say it would be kind of boring, wouldn't you? Does he love you, do you think?'

'Yes. I think he does. *Did*.'

'Did he tell you?'

'Yes.'

Sky's eyebrows shot skyward. 'Wow, I'm impressed,' she murmured thoughtfully. 'It takes guts for a guy to confess his love, you know? So if he told you that, I reckon he won't have changed his mind in the space of a few weeks.'

Brie prided herself on understanding men but she'd never looked further than skin-deep. Except with Leo. Every time she'd started looking beyond their initial attraction, she'd pushed such thoughts away.

She'd not thanked him as he deserved to be thanked for the fire alarms she'd given him such grief about. His efforts at organising her garden shed—who'd go to all that trouble for someone else unless they were really special to them? And she'd repaid him with the kind of appalling social skills she'd accused him of having. She'd refused to view it in the way she should have.

Because she was a coward.

She wiped the lotion off of Sky's fingers with a damp

towel. Maybe, as Sky said, Leo just needed to be needed—
Hang on a bit. Brie frowned. 'How did you know it was
only a few weeks ago?'

Sky regarded her a moment, then said, 'Because Leo
Hamilton's my brother and I can't stand seeing him so
unhappy.'

Stunned into silence, Brie stared at Sky while confused
thoughts raced through her head. Finally, she managed,
'But his sister's name's—'

'Yeah. Sunny-Sky. Hyphenated.' She shrugged, gave
a small smile. 'Mum thought it was cute. And Camp-
bell's her maiden name. I apologise for the deception but
I wanted to meet this special woman Leo's so hung up on.
He doesn't know I'm here, by the way, so if we can keep
this between—'

'Leo's unhappy?' Why did that make Brie feel so much
better?

'I haven't seen much of him lately. He's given himself a
massive workload this past week, but we had lunch yesterday and his mood wasn't pretty. Still, he talked, and for a
guy like Leo that's a way big deal. And this control thing
he's got going on? Pretty irritating, believe me, I know.
But it stems from our childhood. Why don't you call him?'

'I don't think he'll—'

'Yes—he will. Trust me. Better yet, trust him.'

CHAPTER THIRTEEN

AFTER FALLING INTO bed at midnight, Brie woke again at just after one in the morning. Sleep was impossible with so much stuff spinning around inside her head. She went downstairs, made a mug of warm milk and honey, her favourite comfort food, then carried it to the living room. Snuggling into a comfy armchair, she switched on the wall furnace and warmed her bare toes while she sipped.

Sunny-Sky's surprise visit had knocked Brie sideways and she was still reeling. Brie had to admire her for having the guts to pull off such a stunt. The simple pretext had been for a noble reason and Brie knew she'd always intended coming clean before leaving. It showed Brie just how much love existed between the siblings and had given Brie a new insight into the man who'd stolen her heart.

And unexpectedly enough, into herself.

Sunny, as she preferred to be called, had held a mirror up to Brie's doubts and questions and fears and insecurities. She'd forced Brie to look deeply and honestly at herself—and she acknowledged it was way past time.

She didn't like what she saw.

Because her father's decisions and choices had had such a negative impact on her life, her motives and the way she'd conducted herself where Leo was concerned were a coward's way. Time to change that.

To trust him.

Sunny's powerful words swept away some of Brie's insecurities. Leo was nothing like her father. But her insides were churning as she pulled a note pad off the coffee table. She wanted to show him once and for all that she was ready to take that risk he'd told her to think about. The one she'd been too afraid to take a few weeks ago. If only she wasn't too late…

The following morning, Brie waited until she had a break between clients to ring Leo. Heart pounding into her throat, she waited for him to answer. What if she'd taken too long to get back to him? What if he saw her name and ignored her call? No, that was Brie's MO.

'Breanna, good morning. This is a surprise—and a co-incidence.'

Oh? At the familiar sound of his deep voice, she gripped the phone tighter. 'Good morning, Leo.' How formal. How stilted. How wrong given what they'd been to one another. 'A coincidence?'

'I was going to call you today with an idea. But firstly, how have you been?'

'Fine.' She hesitated then told the truth. 'Not fine.'

'Sorry to hear that.'

He didn't sound sorry. He sounded pleased. She squeezed her eyes shut and said, 'What were you going to call me about?'

'We'll start with why you called me.'

'I have a favour to ask—it's not urgent.' His reason might affect her plans. 'You?'

'It's essentially a business call.'

She ignored the stab of disappointment and said, 'How can I help?'

'I've been giving the Pink Snowflake Foundation a lot of thought. I have a proposal you might be interested in.'

Not that kind of proposal, Brie. 'I'm always interested in anything that supports Pink Snowflake.'

'I'd like to discuss it with you, hear your opinion. We'll keep it business.'

'Definitely. Business.'

'Would tomorrow suit? Five o'clock, at your salon?'

It couldn't have worked out better if she'd organised his meeting herself. 'I have a late client so I'd prefer six. But I've got something happening after.' She hoped.

'Okay.' His tone was brisk. 'Six o'clock. I'll see you then.'

Brie was ready and waiting when Leo tapped on her open office door at precisely six the following evening. Without thought, she lifted her hand to check the formal knot of hair on the top of her head. 'Good evening, Leo. Come in.'

'Evening, Brie.'

She wasn't quite ready for her heart-racing response to his use of her informal name. Nor was she prepared for the sight of his masculine allure in his charcoal suit and snowy shirt and neat-as-a-pin maroon tie. 'Dressed to impress,' she said. 'And I am. Impressed, that is.' And rushed on with, 'This must be an important proposal. *Business* proposal.'

'It is,' he said, voice as crisp as a dress shirt.

Brie bit her lip. Leo had always had that destabilising effect on her. Beneath her black buttoned-up jacket she was anything but the cool, calm, in-control woman she wanted to be with him tonight.

Then it hit her and she wanted to die of humiliation and embarrassment. He hadn't suited up for her. He was dressed for some social function or other—which more than likely included female company—and was simply calling past here on the way. *Great going, Brie.* He wasn't the only one who jumped to the wrong conclusions.

He stepped into the tiny room, which wasn't much bigger than a closet. He cocked his head as if to ask if she usually wore a business jacket in her line of work, then his gaze drifted lower to the short hemline of her shiny new party dress and he said nothing. Just lifted his eyes back to her face. For an instant, she saw his eyes darken with emotions she couldn't guess at, yet he'd laid it all out for her not so long ago. For a few brief shiny moments she'd seen the real Leo Hamilton.

She missed that man.

Her glimmering red dress and the sophisticated hair was all part of the plan to win that man back. She sat on her stool, indicated an office chair she'd brought from the shared lunch room, and invited him to have a seat.

He did, while looking at the mess sprawled over most of her desk which was pushed up against one wall.

'I know.' She looked him straight in those enigmatic silver eyes. 'I didn't thank you for tidying up my garden. And my books. And the kitchen. I was rude and I apologise.'

'You're welcome. Sometimes I came on too strong.'

She smiled. 'I'm getting used to the way it works with you. With us. Maybe I can start again, put the messy bits behind me...'

He didn't react the way she'd hoped and barbed wire tightened around her heart. She realised, now, that she wanted that life he'd offered her, and she was willing to risk everything for it. She wanted to tell him she loved him back. If he hadn't changed his mind. Even if he had.

He got straight down to business. 'The reason I'm here is to suggest a fundraiser for Pink Snowflake. I'm asking Hope Strings to do a charity performance and they're more than happy to donate their time for a worthy cause. I thought an evening with fine music, dining and dancing. So I've booked the classiest venue in Hobart—it's Sunrise-Sunset on the fourteenth of June.'

She blinked while she caught up. 'You've gone ahead and booked Sunrise-Sunset. Without asking me?'

'The thing is,' he said slowly, resolutely, 'I admire Pink Snowflake's vision and I intend to proceed with my fund-raising idea with or without you. Having said that, I'd love to have you work alongside me on this.'

He was pledging himself to the cause dearest to her heart and was willing to go ahead with his plans alone if necessary. 'Of course I want to be involved. Tell me more.'

He smiled. 'Thought you'd say that. Eight weeks should be enough time to get organised. I'm thinking a glittering event with a couple of big-name Aussie celebrities I can call on at short notice.'

'I'm in. Glittering events are my forte.' She clapped her hands together, brought them to her lips to keep her smile from flying away. She still had a chance. 'One thing, though. Hope Strings is classical. What about those of us who like to shake their booty on a dance floor?'

'Don't worry, Hope Strings is nothing if not versatile. There'll be plenty of time for dirty dancing.'

She did a little finger clap in front of her lips. 'Excellent.'

He glanced at the clock on her wall, shifted on his chair as if in a hurry to leave. 'There was a favour you wanted to ask me?'

'It can wait.' Actually, no. It couldn't. She had to tell him now, before he walked out of here in his special suit and tie for his maybe special date. Sunny had told her Leo was a man who needed to be needed. 'I need someone who lives and breathes organisation. You know someone like that?'

He nodded once. 'I'm your man.'

'The office needs some structure before I relocate it to the McPherson retreat.' She waved an encompassing hand. 'If you could, maybe, help me create some order out of the chaos some time soon, I'd be very grateful.'

'How grateful?'

'Very.' He watched her for a moment without answering, his expression giving nothing away.

She wished she knew what he'd meant by that question. She wished she knew what he thought *she* meant. Because honestly? She didn't mean it in a sexual way. She'd be grateful for any contact, no matter how fleeting.

'I'll do it,' he said at last. 'As a special favour to you.' He spoke casually, his long-fingered hands on his knees. 'You want to work with me on it?'

'Not necessary.' She breathed a sigh of relief and optimism. 'I trust you to do an amazing job. You can even organise your own filing system, so long as you teach me how to use it.' It was her turn to glance at her diamond watch. Her plan was still on schedule. 'I'll put the date for the fundraiser in my diary and we'll make another time to go over the details, but right now I've got something more important happening.'

She rose, watching his eyes darken as she unbuttoned her jacket and took it off. She tossed it onto her desk, slid open her top desk drawer and pulled out a glitzy evening purse.

Leo's eyes didn't know where to look first. At the silky fabric clinging to her womanly curves, or the long legs encased in shimmery stockings or the spiked heels on her feet.

Her strapless fire-engine-red dress enhanced her toned shoulders and prominent collarbones; the upswept hair revealed her slender neck to perfection.

'I'm not the only one dressed to impress,' he murmured, lifting his hungry eyes to her jewelled midnight ones, struggling hard not to let possessiveness get the upper hand.

He wanted to beat his chest and roar to the world that she was his, and only his. He wanted to reach out, loosen her hair and let the silken strands tumble into his hands. He wanted to yank her to him and hold her prisoner until she yielded to him and admitted what he already knew in his heart and wanted to hear aloud—that she loved him.

Or had he got it spectacularly wrong?

'Looks like it's some party you've got lined up.'

'It is.' She opened her purse and drew out the necklace he'd given her in Singapore, held it out. 'I was having trouble with the clasp. Will you do this up for me?' She turned.

'So you've decided to keep it.'

'Yes.'

Clenching his jaw, he performed the task even though the tiny rational part that was left of his brain told him to get the hell out before he made an idiot of himself. Again. Why was he letting her play him for a fool?

Never more a fool than a man in crazy, impossible love.

She turned back, the diamonds glittering at her throat, her eyes focused on his. She pressed the intercom. 'Jodie, thanks. That'll be all. I'll see you tomorrow.'

His cue to leave too? 'I'll get going, then.'

'There's something else I need you to do,' she said softly. 'Do you trust me? I trust you. *I trust you, Leo Hamilton.*'

He stared into her fathomless eyes and saw hope. He nodded, because frankly he wasn't sure he could get his voice to work.

He followed her out of her office to her treatment room, hardly daring to look at the stunning vision in front of him. She stopped at the closed door, pressed her lips together and turned to look at him. For the first time, her heart was in her eyes. Unguarded, open, still so achingly vulnerable.

'If you had plans for tonight, I don't care how important they were, cancel them.'

He'd made none but said, 'Consider them cancelled.'

She nodded, then murmured, 'One party coming up,' and pushed the door open. Dozens of tea-lights flickered on all available surfaces, giving the room an intimate golden glow. A bottle of bubbly chilled on a pedestal in the corner. And all he could think to say was, 'You left these candles burning unattended?'

Her laugh was a full-throated sound of genuine amusement. And no candle could shine brighter than Brie's smile, which lit up her face like he'd never seen.

'Would I do that? No, Jodie kept an eye out till I was ready, so zip that totally kissable mouth of yours and let me do the talking. I remembered you liked parties for two, so here we are. There's a rule though: there'll be no sex here.'

His brows rose. 'No sex?' He saw the sunshine in her eyes—and the clouds of uncertainty beneath. He tsk-tsked. 'That's a bad rule, Brie.'

She tapped his lips. 'And no interruptions till I say so.'

He set his lips against the intercepting fingers and nodded.

She paced away a little then turned to him. 'You were right when you accused me of hiding the real Brie from the world. I've spent my life perfecting the art and it's a form of lying—you were right about that too. I've been lying to myself. I've been playing in a world I thought I wanted, free to please myself but ending my relationships before they got serious. And I really thought I was happy.'

She shook her head. 'Not any more. I've realised that true freedom comes not from a long list of casual, meaningless acquaintances but with an honest, open commitment to one. So I want to thank you. Very much. I'm free because of you. I understand myself—even if no one else does.

'I'm not bound by fear of "what-if", because I've learned to trust. To trust *you*. That night when you came to me with your story and your heart and soul in your words, you showed me it's safe to fall in love.'

'Brie—'

'Please, don't interrupt.' She held up a hand. 'I need to get it out. My parents were totally focused on their own misery. They threw gifts and money at me and hoped I'd go away and leave them alone. I felt abandoned and invisible. So I partied, rebelled and garnered often inappropriate attention but at least it was attention—just for all the wrong reasons. And I've already told you about Elliot.

'Which is why I viewed your flowers as an easy apology for standing me up, and I apologise because no one should come before your sister. The diamonds...' she touched the sparkling jewels at her neck '...brought back the bad old days.'

'Enough.' Two steps and he was in front of her, brushing loose hair from her brow, kissing away her hurts, soothing away her fears. 'Enough. Relax, breathe. You're shivering.' He rubbed her upper arms.

'I'm not cold, just emotional. It's okay.' Brie could barely see through the veil of tears. She'd never felt so treasured, so safe as she did in that moment. And her entire body was indeed shivering.

With sheer paralysing fear of what he'd say next.

'I love you too,' she said, determined to finish what she'd started. 'And I want to spend the rest of my life with you. If it's not too late. So I have a proposal of my own.' She reached into her purse and pulled out a black velvet box, pushed it into his hand. 'I'm asking you to marry me.'

His eyebrows rose. 'You're proposing marriage to me?'

'Isn't that what people want to do when they love each other? Show their commitment? Announce to the whole world that they're officially off the market?' Her breath rushed out and embarrassing despair rushed in to fill its place. Her cheeks burned. 'Oh, *no*. Stupid, stupid me. You don't want to get married. I am *such* an idiot. Of course you don't. Why would you?'

She tried to snatch her box back but his fist tightened

around it. 'No. You don't give someone a gift then take it back. Didn't anyone tell you it's bad manners?'

'I never gave a man a gift before. Except Jett, and that first time didn't go so well. And this…this isn't…' She trailed off beneath his gaze.

His eyes looked deep into hers, so deep, she felt the love from them touch her soul. Then he said, 'Let's open it, shall we?'

'I…' She pressed her lips together as he flipped the lid open.

His mouth kicked up at one corner. 'Well, now.' With great care and a million stuttering heartbeats later, he lifted the ring out of its box. The cluster of rubies and diamonds winked in the candlelight. He slid it onto the tip of his pinkie and shook his head. 'It doesn't fit me. You'll have to wear it.'

He lifted his eyes to hers and smiled. 'What do you say?'

Thank you? No. She batted his chest. 'You're confusing me; it's what do *you* say.'

'I say I love you right back and let's get married.' He slid the ring onto her left finger. 'It suits your bright and shiny personality. And it's stunning, just like you. But I'll pay for it.'

'No, no, no.'

'I insist. No pay, no marriage contract.'

'You can buy an eternity ring for our first wedding anniversary.'

'I'll buy that too.'

She settled against his chest. 'Since you insist, I'll let you win. This time.'

'Deal.' Leo sealed it with a kiss, then swept her off her feet and up, before blowing out candles.

'What are you doing?'

'I want to make love to you and you've said this place

is off-limits so I'm taking you home.' He swung past the ice bucket. 'Grab that bottle of bubbly.'

'Home?'

He kissed her as he carried her to the door. 'To West Wind.'

Hours later, Leo awoke. They lay together, their limbs entwined in the dimness. Brie had agreed to share his Melbourne house on occasional weekends, and he'd be there when he worked in Victoria, but they were making their home West Wind. She'd even agreed to let Mrs J come over and keep house for them. With her heavy workload and commitments to Pink Snowflake, he knew Brie needed someone to help, and Mrs J was more than keen.

He turned his head on the pillow and watched her sleeping. Her breasts were warm and soft against his chest, and his erection was nudging her hip. He rolled over, pinning her beneath him and stroking her hair from her face. 'Wake up, baby doll.'

Sleepy eyes opened, her full inviting lips curved. 'I wasn't asleep. I was thinking.'

He cupped a breast, rolled the nipple between thumb and forefinger. 'About this?'

Her smile widened against his roaming lips. 'About your constant need to be on top of things.'

'I let you be on top last time.'

'You did,' she agreed. 'But it's not sex I'm talking about right now, Mr Must-stay-in-control-at-all-times Hamilton.' Wriggling out from beneath him and rolling onto her side, she propped her head on her elbow and studied him in the semi-darkness. 'Did you thank Sunny, or give her a lecture about interfering in your love life?'

'Sunny? What do you mean?'

'She didn't tell you?'

Brie looked so horrified, he bit back a smile. 'Tell me what?'

'That she came to see me at the salon.'

'When was this?'

'Oh.' She rolled onto her back. 'I think I just messed up a beautiful sibling relationship.'

'You mean when Sunny-Sky went to extraordinary lengths to beg you to give me a chance?' His hand found and stroked her belly button.

'Yes.' She visibly relaxed. 'Sunny-Sky. You weren't mad?'

'Why would I be? She convinced you I was the one, didn't she?' He touched her little piercing. 'Why a strawberry?'

'My sixteen-year-old self's little rebellion. My parents hated body decoration. And I love strawberries. They're pretty and dainty and they taste sweet.'

'Since you possess all three attributes, it suits you perfectly.'

She snorted. 'I thought we were going to be honest with each other?'

'Okay, maybe dainty's—'

'Fine, if you think it suits me, I'm happy.'

'So am I.' He spread his hand over her flat belly. Would they ever have their own children? He hoped so. 'You know something? Mum would have loved you. Almost as much as I do.'

Her smile was brilliant against the dimness. 'See? Easy. I don't need flowers and fancy gifts, just the words. Just the love. And I adore you right back.'

EPILOGUE

THE SUNRISE-SUNSET ballroom was a glittering collision of sensory delights. Rainbows bounced off glassware and jewels sparkled beneath chandeliers dripping crystals. Hope Strings entertained with a selection of Vivaldi and Purcell while the guests, who'd paid big bucks to attend, enjoyed canapés including such delicacies as chicken and coriander dumplings, lemon-myrtle-dusted fish goujons with tartare sauce and lobster onion pâté with lavoche, to be followed throughout the evening by three more courses of equally sumptuous fare.

Brie saw her brother—a head taller than everyone else bar the man at her side—near the window overlooking the harbour and glimpsed Olivia's flaming red hair alongside. 'They're here,' she told Leo and, grabbing his hand, she tugged him through the crowd.

The four of them had caught up a month ago when Jett and Olivia had returned from their honeymoon, and the newlyweds were almost as excited as Brie and Leo about the upcoming wedding.

Jett's face lit when he turned and saw her heading towards him. 'Hey, Brie.'

Brie would never get sick of her big brother's smile. 'Hey, there, yourself.' She hugged Jett first, then turned to Olivia. 'How are you feeling today, honey?'

'Not bad *now*. Pretty awful for the rest of the day.'

Livvy looked amazing, as usual, but there were smudges beneath her eyes. There was a reason for that and it made Brie smile. 'How's my little niece or nephew coming along in there?' Brie patted the small mound covered in sky-blue silk.

'It's a he,' Olivia muttered. 'A female would never give me such a hard time. Don't let me put you off having babies though.'

Brie smiled up at Leo. 'As if.' She hugged his arm. 'Just not yet though.'

Olivia grimaced. 'That's what I said and look at me.' She glared at her husband, who just shrugged as if he'd had nothing to do with it.

Brie slung an arm around Jett. 'Go on, you were both thrilled. Did you purchase that little cradle you were looking at?'

'Yes.' Livvy's expression brightened. 'And while we were there we saw some adorable wallpaper with teddies.'

Leo exchanged a look with Jett and raised his glass. 'Anyone for a refill?'

Talk of cradles and babies obviously made Brie's future husband uneasy and she smiled to herself.

Jett jerked a thumb. 'There's a guy over there who wants to talk to you about his environmental concerns on the north-west coast, if you've got a minute.'

Brie caught Jett's glint of humour directed her way then watched the two most important guys in her life merge into the crowd. She smiled and turned to Olivia. 'How's Jett with all this baby talk?'

'He's as thrilled as me, he just doesn't want to show it in public. So Eve's Naturally is doing okay?'

Brie's business had moved to the McPherson retreat last month. 'We're almost on track after Leo's hard work with the filing system.' Brie groaned. 'I swear I didn't inherit the organisational gene.'

'You don't need to—you have a slave at your beck and call now.'

Brie laughed. 'Don't let him hear you say that.'

Hours later, the Blue Menagerie jazz band provided an easy syncopated beat and Leo got Brie onto the dance floor, more as an excuse to have her up close than to dance. Sunny and Gregor were taking a well-deserved break near the orchestra and waved as Leo guided Brie past.

He loved whatever she wore but tonight she looked extra special. She was wearing the dress she'd proposed to him in. A grin twitched at the corner of his mouth. And it wasn't even a leap year...

'See? I *am* capable of allowing a man to lead on the dance floor,' she told him, batting her lashes coquettishly.

'And I'm thinking of lying back in bed and letting you do all the work tonight,' he replied.

She looked at her watch in mock surprise. 'Goodness, it's getting late. We should go. Now.'

'Not so fast.' He tugged her closer, ran his hands over her bare shoulder blades. 'It's nice, holding you like this.' They moved slowly to the music, wrapped in each other's arms and lost in the moment. 'Don't ever change, baby doll. You're perfect just as you are.'

'That goes for you too.' She smoothed his lapel and stared up at him. 'We'll have that for our wedding waltz.'

'Have what?'

'Billy Joel's "Just the Way You Are".'

'We'll make a list and vote on them.'

'Okay. So long as we both vote for Billy.'

'One thing's for sure, we're going to take forever to get bored.'

She pressed her lips to his chin. 'Sounds perfect to me.'

* * * * *

Mills & Boon® Hardback

September 2014

ROMANCE

The Housekeeper's Awakening	Sharon Kendrick
More Precious than a Crown	Carol Marinelli
Captured by the Sheikh	Kate Hewitt
A Night in the Prince's Bed	Chantelle Shaw
Damaso Claims His Heir	Annie West
Changing Constantinou's Game	Jennifer Hayward
The Ultimate Revenge	Victoria Parker
Tycoon's Temptation	Trish Morey
The Party Dare	Anne Oliver
Sleeping with the Soldier	Charlotte Phillips
All's Fair in Lust & War	Amber Page
Dressed to Thrill	Bella Frances
Interview with a Tycoon	Cara Colter
Her Boss by Arrangement	Teresa Carpenter
In Her Rival's Arms	Alison Roberts
Frozen Heart, Melting Kiss	Ellie Darkins
After One Forbidden Night...	Amber McKenzie
Dr Perfect on Her Doorstep	Lucy Clark

MEDICAL

A Secret Shared...	Marion Lennox
Flirting with the Doc of Her Dreams	Janice Lynn
The Doctor Who Made Her Love Again	Susan Carlisle
The Maverick Who Ruled Her Heart	Susan Carlisle

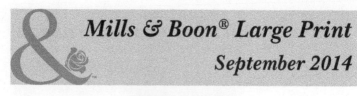

Mills & Boon® Large Print

September 2014

ROMANCE

The Only Woman to Defy Him	Carol Marinelli
Secrets of a Ruthless Tycoon	Cathy Williams
Gambling with the Crown	Lynn Raye Harris
The Forbidden Touch of Sanguardo	Julia James
One Night to Risk it All	Maisey Yates
A Clash with Cannavaro	Elizabeth Power
The Truth About De Campo	Jennifer Hayward
Expecting the Prince's Baby	Rebecca Winters
The Millionaire's Homecoming	Cara Colter
The Heir of the Castle	Scarlet Wilson
Twelve Hours of Temptation	Shoma Narayanan

HISTORICAL

Unwed and Unrepentant	Marguerite Kaye
Return of the Prodigal Gilvry	Ann Lethbridge
A Traitor's Touch	Helen Dickson
Yield to the Highlander	Terri Brisbin
Return of the Viking Warrior	Michelle Styles

MEDICAL

Waves of Temptation	Marion Lennox
Risk of a Lifetime	Caroline Anderson
To Play with Fire	Tina Beckett
The Dangers of Dating Dr Carvalho	Tina Beckett
Uncovering Her Secrets	Amalie Berlin
Unlocking the Doctor's Heart	Susanne Hampton

Mills & Boon® Hardback
October 2014

ROMANCE

An Heiress for His Empire	Lucy Monroe
His for a Price	Caitlin Crews
Commanded by the Sheikh	Kate Hewitt
The Valquez Bride	Melanie Milburne
The Uncompromising Italian	Cathy Williams
Prince Hafiz's Only Vice	Susanna Carr
A Deal Before the Altar	Rachael Thomas
Rival's Challenge	Abby Green
The Party Starts at Midnight	Lucy King
Your Bed or Mine?	Joss Wood
Turning the Good Girl Bad	Avril Tremayne
Breaking the Bro Code	Stefanie London
The Billionaire in Disguise	Soraya Lane
The Unexpected Honeymoon	Barbara Wallace
A Princess by Christmas	Jennifer Faye
His Reluctant Cinderella	Jessica Gilmore
One More Night with Her Desert Prince...	Jennifer Taylor
From Fling to Forever	Avril Tremayne

MEDICAL

It Started with No Strings...	Kate Hardy
Flirting with Dr Off-Limits	Robin Gianna
Dare She Date Again?	Amy Ruttan
The Surgeon's Christmas Wish	Annie O'Neil

Mills & Boon® Large Print

October 2014

ROMANCE

HISTORICAL

MEDICAL

MILLS & BOON®

Why shop at millsandboon.co.uk?

Each year, thousands of romance readers find their perfect read at millsandboon.co.uk. That's because we're passionate about bringing you the very best romantic fiction. Here are some of the advantages of shopping at www.millsandboon.co.uk:

* **Get new books first**—you'll be able to buy your favourite books one month before they hit the shops

* **Get exclusive discounts**—you'll also be able to buy our specially created monthly collections, with up to 50% off the RRP

* **Find your favourite authors**—latest news, interviews and new releases for all your favourite authors and series on our website, plus ideas for what to try next

* **Join in**—once you've bought your favourite books, don't forget to register with us to rate, review and join in the discussions

Visit **www.millsandboon.co.uk**
for all this and more today!